I0692118

Praise For

THE HOUSE ON THE BEND

The characters just jump off the page! They are compellingly complex and exceedingly relatable. Reach has an uncanny ability to wrap the reader up in their world. This coming-of-age story reminds us of the power of love, and that we are never too far gone to be changed by it. Eagerly awaiting the screenplay!

—**Hannah Mwangi,** Author of *Just Because We're Different*, Artist, Educator.

***

With this raw, emotional, passionate storyline, M.E. Reach will have you unable to put the book down. *The House on the Bend* is a story about guilt, shame, reconciliation, and the grace and mercy of Jesus Christ. A story everyone can relate to in one thing or another, and something every believer should read at least once.

—**Rhonda Wheeler,** Social Media Manager, B.S. English

***

The House on the Bend captures the messiness of humanity in such a raw way. The authentic struggle to do what is right...is illustrated and the significant impact of relationships with others on our lives is emphasized. Long after the last page has been turned, the characters will live on; especially, as I imagine a day when I'll be brave enough to go to the top of a Ferris wheel, too!

—**Dr. Rebecca Estes,** Hoosier Educator, Passionate Reader.

THE HOUSE
ON THE BEND

M.E. REACH

Published by KHARIS PUBLISHING, an imprint of
KHARIS MEDIA LLC.

Copyright © 2024 M. E. Reach

ISBN-13: 978-1-63746-264-5

ISBN-10: 1-63746-264-6

Library of Congress Control Number: 2024946459

Unless otherwise indicated, Scripture quotations are taken from:

All KHARIS PUBLISHING products are available at special
quantity discounts for bulk purchase for sales promotions,
premiums, fund-raising, and educational needs. For details,
contact:
Kharis Media LLC
Tel: 1-630-909-3405
support@kharispublishing.com
www.kharispublishing.com

CONTENTS

SATURDAY NIGHT

He'd closed his eyes for 'bout the hundredth time waitin' on the swimmin' feelin' to subside. It hadn't been the first time the room started spinnin' for no good reason, aside from the obvious bottles linin' the countertop. But this was different. Felt different. This time the music an' the company hadn't hushed the naggin' he felt there somewhere underneath it all. He couldn't quite put his finger on it, but it was like his fingers felt numb, like wakin' from a dream that felt real as a heart attack, only nothin' had changed...nothin'. The cold, refreshin' touch of the bottle didn't cool 'em, an' the sound of the cans crunchin' didn't make music in his ears. Sounded silly, which was why he never said such a thing, but the truth was the truth no matter how dumb it all sounded.

He almost laughed at how weird it all felt, but he couldn't muster the smirk to even grin.

Jus' felt downright pitiful an' empty. Worse. Like that feelin' you get when you're doin' dishes an' yer hand slides in the empty pickle jar, an' you try to slip it back out, but it ain't fittin'. The way everything had begun in his life seemed so much easier than it did now. Simple. So simple he hadn't even thought 'bout what might happen if he got stuck.

But now it was too late, an' his life wasn't workin' its way out like it ought.

It was there, with everything spinnin' 'round an' in the middle o' the mess, he sorta quit tryin' an' closed his eyes thinkin' 'bout everything that'd happened, an' what made today any more special than any other day. He tossed his arms up on the counter an' curled 'em round then let his head fall in the middle like they used to when he was a kid in school an' they'd play that ol' game, Head's Up Seven Up. Man, he loved that game. The thought stopped the world from spinnin' for a hot minute, but not long enough to keep it stuck. Maybe, if he tried hard enough, he could make a trade. He could sit there really still an' let the world around him spin back an' take him to the days of jus' the two of 'em before any of this mess happened? Maybe he could hold her again, or gaze into those pretty blue eyes squintin' in the sunlight. Hear a laugh or two?

Let's go back, he heard a thought. *I'll take you back.*

He wanted to fight it, but he couldn't. The dog in him didn't wanna fight anymore.

Let's go back, he agreed. *Show me how to go back. Show me how to fix it.*

1

IN THE PORCH LIGHT

SATURDAY

U p and to the left, past the sign that read *Hidden Drive*. Davis had taken the curve a million times since he got his lil' green truck two years ago. Now all he could do was stare at his hard-earned money smoking sidelong, all wonky in the red clay of a Mississippi ditch.

"Son of a…"

A light popped on in the window of the house. Up, on what looked like a hill by Mississippi standards, stood an old yella house with mismatched shingles on it. The shed next to it had a rusted tin roof shimmerin' in the porch light from where he stood. Old Highway 67 didn't have many streetlights. Whoever it was likely couldn't see him from where they'd looked when they heard the crash, an' were eager to take a closer look.

Run, he thought, but what'd be the use? Ain't like his truck would disappear an' magically reappear behind the old man's shop anyhow. An' if it did, most of them would trash it an' sell it fer parts before he could blink. All Davis could do was sigh an' run a hand beneath his hat, mopping the sweat slippin' down his brow to blend with the blond on top. An old woman crept out a few seconds later, snatchin' the ends of the belt on her bathrobe. A sigh of relief snuck out. *At least it wasn't an old man*, he thought.

"You aight, boy?" she called.

"Yes'am," he said.

"Anybody else in 'ere?"

"No, ma'am,"

"Done wrecked it good, huh?" she said as much as asked. "You's movin', too. Yer dang near half up the drive."

He glanced back to the ditch an' where it curved. The old rotten fence hadn't done a thing, practically disintegrated. The house didn't look much better from where he stood, but it *was* dark.

"Need a phone?"

"No ma'am," he said. "I done called somebody ta come get me," he lied. "Ought ta be here soon. Sorry 'bout this."

"Tha' turn gets lots a folks. An' yer sure you don't need nothin'? Wanna come sit on the porch while ya wait?"

"No, ma'am. Thank ya though. There's a deer," he lied with a point to the curve.

She nodded. "*Hmm*, well, a'ight then."

As if God himself was calling his bluff, a nasty bile burp slid up his throat. He fought to hold it down. *That'd be another thing*, he knew. He needed to clean the cans up out of his truck somehow before his old man saw 'em. He wasn't sure which one was worse, being caught drinkin', or the fact he'd been drivin' way too fast, but at least one might hold up if he stuck to the deer story.

An old Mountain Dew bottle in the cab rolled into his hands not long after he tossed the fourth or fifth can in the Walmart baggie. There's *just* enough in it to use like mouthwash an' cologne. Sticky, but enough. With a glance to the porch to make sure the old lady hadn't wandered back out, he stomped on it a few times to crush them all down, so they'd fit, then tossed it near the drain in the ditch. It'd blend in with all the others up an' down the highway. Most folks tossed their trash in the country, especially around the curves. More than a few beer bottles had met the *Hidden Drive* sign by the looks of the shattered glass on the ground.

Davis didn't notice the other window on the side of the house, or the blinds ease back into place from where they'd bent. The light hadn't been on in that window.

His old man showed up with a snarl that'd make milk curdle. Davis stayed in Ol' Pearl while he walked up the drive and spoke to the old lady a bit, pointin' here an' there with a chuckle. They were a little too far away to make out the words, but everything seemed smooth enough. He'd been more thankful she hadn't called the highway patrol on him. He'd been toast then. Half of Davis hoped the old man's spirits might be different when he came back down the gravel drive, but the other half knew better. His smile slid to a scowl as the porch light passed from his face, like watchin' somethin' out-a scary movie.

"Ain't gonna get it tonight," he said. "It'll wait 'til the mornin'."

Fifteen minutes felt like a slow, silent death. He'd rather have a lecture than nothin' at all. Not even the radio. Davis thought to sneak his hand up and tap the knob, but couldn't muster up the kahunas. He'd drank enough liquid courage to be sure, but most of that'd worn off thanks to the fear of it all. To say the old man was ticked would've been an understatement, but he did seem a bit relieved at the sight of the truck and the fact Davis had walked away without so much as a scratch. Didn't even question the deer story, neither

Tossed their keys in the dish after they'd kicked off their boots and put 'em on the rack, quick to step inside before the little frogs on the side of the trailer under the porch light could pop in the screen door. The old man breathed a sigh, shakin' his head like he always did whenever Davis did somethin' boneheaded. It was either too early ta nag him, or he's too tired, Davis didn't know which, but he didn't plan on complainin' about it.

"D'you," Davis started to speak, but a hand silenced him.

"Jus' get ta bed, turd head," he said solemnly. "I'll holler at ya in the mornin'. Well," he glanced to the clock. "...*later* in the mornin'."

Once the door shut to Davis' room, the old man sighed again, shakin' his head. His feet slid more than walked cross the worn linoleum to the fridge. He stared in, wantin' something ta drink, but not really. At first, his head had been spinnin', remindin' him all over again about the night the patrolman knocked on the door an' gave him the news. Suddenly, he's dog-tired, again. He couldn't rightly ask for the day off —not with all those young bucks in their button-down shirts barkin' at the old fellas. An' he sure didn't want any of the other newbies an' their shiny tools sneakin' up to his spot, either. A hand strayed toward one of the cans on the shelf to put his nerves at ease, but a second thought brought it back empty-handed.

Nah, he thought. He saw the patrolman under porch light in his mind, again. How he took off his hat with a solemn nod before he broke the news all those years ago on a night much like this one.

Y'all 've done enough damage fer one night, he decided as he shut the fridge with a scowl. Without another thought, the old man shook his head again and slid his feet along the floor to his bed. Tomorrow was gonna be a long day.

2

IN THE DARKNESS

SATURDAY

Spring Break shut down the beaches an' jammed up the traffic up an' down Highway 49, but the thump of the bass and the endless honkin' couldn't be heard wherever they were now. Both guys were kissin' on her in the backseat. At first, only the lil' man had been with her, but when they stopped an' got some gas, the big guy in the passenger seat hopped back there, too. She only saw the squinty eyes of the driver in the rear-view mirror – the same ones that pretended not to see or hear whenever she whined for them to stop grabbin' at her so much.

There's nothin' Jewel could do though, between the two of 'em. She'd liked it at first, but when the car started spinnin' and the lights on the road became blurry, somethin' didn't seem right. Her arms got weaker, sluggish like they's fallin' asleep. The words of Shayla echoed in her head before she got on the bus two days ago.

Girl, you gonna get drugged and kilt. It's Mississippi, girl!

"Don't you know that only happens in the movies?" Jewels had said. "You 'bout dumb! Besides, the outhern boys cain't handle this."

Mmm-hmm, Shayla sounded. Jewels could still see her half-pouty lips an' those eyebrows on-point as Shay stared at her like she was watchin' her now. The men felt like they had more hands than they should.

"Who's dumb now?" Shayla's eyes asked all over again.

It'd been the only time she'd ever left Indy since she moved there before she could remember, an' by the time the car finally stopped an' they opened the door and dumped her out on the side of the road, she wondered if she'd ever see it, again.

~*~

Paige crossed her arms with a fake pout.

"Hey, Liam," she said sweetly. Her big blue eyes cut at 'em somethin' fierce but he shook the thought away. The other two beside her had matching hazel and brown ones. Liam rolled his eyes and glanced to the door of the office with a look that begged Mr. Montgomery to scowl and say no, but as usual he didn't. With a grin as wide as the gulf, he waved. This time of year, the managers didn't care how many free rides the workers gave so long as the lines stayed packed, and the tickets kept selling in rolls at the office. Truth be told, Liam half thought the thin old man just liked watchin' him squirm at the girls gushin' over him.

"Aight," Liam said to the approving giggle of the girls. He unlatched the chain and let them on the Tilt-o-Whirl, again. Last week, it'd been the Ferris wheel. The weekend before, it'd been the Bumper Cars. Whichever ride Liam worked, they were there.

"Help me with my strap, again?" Paige asked.

Liam leaned over. She lifted her arms and leaned a little closer as he tucked it around her and then pulled the shoulder-straps forward. He half expected her to kiss him. Seemed like every time she'd lean a lil' closer than the last. *What would he do if she did*, he wondered? That'd make a mess outta things, 'specially come Sunday.

"Me, too, Liam," Katy chimed. "Sorry if it's too much trouble."

"Ain't no trouble," he said with a smile. "These here are a pain ta loosen sometimes," he replied.

Katy touched his arm at the muscle when he yanked on it.

"Not fer you, I'd bet. You're purdy strong."

"Jus' plain purdy," Paige mumbled with another giggle.

Hopefully his hat, the shade of the curved seat-back overshadowing them, and the darkness masked the sight of him blushing. He'd blushed a few times before. It was like chummin' shark infested waters.

The third girl, Cora Lynn, hadn't said anything. She only looked at the floor and blushed when Liam reached for her straps.

"I could do 'em, if ya like?" she said, softly. "Y'ain't gotta..."

"I don't mind, Cora," he replied with a grin. "It's part o' the job. Gotta make ure yer safe."

"You're always makin' sure we're safe, huh, Liam?" another fella's voice called out from the next bucket over. It was Travis, Liam's best friend.

"Hey, Travis!" The girls waved with squinty smiles as Liam stood and worked his way around to the other riders, checking their straps.

"They's sure purdy, Liam," Travis whispered wiggling back against the seat. He was every bit a big as Liam, but a rough fit of seizures when he was young stole a lot of his mind, or so the docs said.

"Yeah, but not as purdy as Miss Nancy," Liam replied. Travis' Sunday school teacher had always been a young crush for the boys ever since Liam had been one. She was barely twenty back then.

"Fancy Nancy," Travis chuckled. "Naw, she's my girl!"

"Not if I snatch her up, first!"

"You ain't gonna," Travis replied with a laugh. He shoved Liam's arm.

"I might."

"You jus' get ta pullin' tha lever," he waved Liam away. "Gotta get tiltin'!"

"Yessir!" Liam said with a pat on the side of the bucket.

Liam started walking home around eleven, after all the rides had been shut down and he mopped the office floor from the arcade games to the punchin' bag. The same punchin' bag he'd let Travis beat him on about fifty times a week. *Eat more vit-a-mins!* It would chant whenever Liam punched it. Travis always laughed at that. He chased him to the truck with a rubber snake while Mr. Montgomery laughed, slapping the steering wheel. Took him a few minutes to calm down and wipe the tears from his eyes before he finally started up the old Ford an' headed out.

"Need a ride, son?" he'd asked, again.

"No, sir...figure I'll walk."

"It's too purdy not to, I suppose," Mr. Montgomery replied with a pat on the door. He pointed a finger-gun at Liam. "Catch ya in the morning, kiddo."

"You bet. "Wouldn't miss it," Liam replied.

The walk home took him through the Mossy Oaks beside Slippery Steve's water park, and further, by the pawn shop an' Sal's Market. By the time he rounded the corner past the bar on the river, the street lights had disappeared altogether. Only stars and the serenading of the bugs and frogs surrounded him. That's when he saw the car stop in the distance and the back door open. Somebody fell out. Liam started forward, but when the door slammed and the car sped off, he broke into a sprint. Whoever it was, wasn't moving. Not even a sound. At first, he thought she was dead.

"Oh, Jesus!" he said over and over. The Big Man answered his prayers. She's breathin'. He looked at her an' lifted her head, hopin' she hadn't cracked it good on the road where they'd tossed her. Who does somethin' like that? He looked back to the bar, but only a pearly white GMC an' a green Chevy remained, an' he recognized those two. There's no way he's gonna leave her with *them*. It was times like these Liam wished he'd given in an' got a phone like everyone else nagged him.

Sure, cause folks toss girls outta their cars like trash all the time 'roun' you, don't they?

The voice taunted him somewhere in the back of his mind. He could only shake his head and hold hers as he brushed a few strands of her pretty purple braids aside and stroked the cold sweat away. Poor thang was nearly naked. There were no police out here, not this far, an' certainly not during Spring Break season. By the looks of things, that'd been where she'd been, too. Her skirt was ripped, an' they hadn't even bothered with putting her shirt back on right. Liam closed it up, then took his thin long-sleeved shirt off and wrapped it around her as he glanced down the road. He made sure to button it up. It looked like a skirt on her, but at least she'd be warm an' 'ave somethin' half-descent on.

Yer 'bout a knucklehead, you know that? he heard Mr. Montgomery say in his mind as his only option became clearer an' clearer.

"Yeah, I know," he mumbled as he used his *'purdy strong arms'*, as Katy often told him, to lift the girl up and carry her. She wasn't nearly as heavy as he thought she might be, but then again, a country mile wasn't short, neither.

3

ALLIE QUAVES

SUNDAY

"**M**ornin' Ms. Luanne," his ol' man said. He had his hat in his hand. Davis could count on one hand how many times he'd seen his pap take his hat off for some*one*. An' those were mostly at funerals. Sure, he took it off when he stepped indoors an' whatnot, an' at the supper table, but outta respect for a person? He couldn't recall.

The shadowy figure eased out from behind the screen door to the porch where she stood just as Davis had seen her earlier, bathrobe an' all.

"Mornin', Robbie," she replied.

Robbie? Davis couldn't believe it. Nobody called the old man by his name, an' those who did wouldn't be breathin' too long if they called him Robbie. Bob, maybe. Robert at doctor's appointments an' whatnot. Bobby'd get a stern glare from the old man. But sure as shootin'), the old man just stood there an' grinned.

"Didn't need to come back first thang. Ain't gonna let nobody get after it. Wanna cup a coffee?" She turned and started back in the door before he could answer.

"Yes'am," he said through the screen. The sound of her slippers slidin' on the floor echoed out around the pines an' turned more than one squirrel's attention away from their chasin'.

"I made some Community. Best there is. You'd better not be one'em Folger boys, an' whoever Max*well* is can keep it at his house far as I'm concerned." She chuckled at her own wit before the sound of the spoon twirled in the cup and the tap on the counter an' the slidin' of her slippers echoed out again.

"Thank ya, Ma'am," he said. Her gaze fell on Davis.

"An look here," she said. "Lil' Davy all big now, drivin'...well, *sorta*...," she chuckled. Davis smirked an' glanced at the porch to the warped wood under his feet.

"Yeah," the old man said, his voice a lil' less chipper now that the reunion boiled down to the reason they's there.

"We ought ta have it outta here 'roun' noon, if tha's aight. I'mma leave him here ta start workin' on yer fence. If he finishes, jus' point an' have 'em do somethin' else."

"He's handy, huh?" she said, a lil' too shocked for Davis' ears.

"Yeah, he's taken ta wood. Been in shop class now past three years of school. Purty handy with a hammer an' some tools fer such a knucklehead."

"Well," she sighed. "Wish I could say I didn't need it, an' be all snoody an' whatnot, but I reckon I won't stare the horse in the mouth. This old bird ain't got what she used ta."

"That's why we build the nests, ain't it?"

"Yessir," she replied. She patted him on the shoulder an' took back the empty cup. "Well, I'll let ya get on ta work. It's good seein' ya. I'll give 'm a bite o' somethin' an' a good boot if he needs 'em."

"Oh, I know. He'll likely need the secon' one more than once."

"These youngin's always do."

The old man opened his mouth, but then closed it an' tossed a hand up as he nodded for Davis to head back toward the truck with him.

"I thought we's jus' gettin' my truck?"

"Thought wrong," he replied. From the backseat he slid out the tool belt and the ol' milk crates with a drill, saw, an' extension cords, and finally the old rusted Folger coffee cans with nails an' screws filled to the brim.

"An' I'm workin', too?" he whined. He hadn't been kiddin' 'bout the *keepin' him busy*...

The ol' man scoffed. "Yeah..."

"Fer free?"

He stopped and eyed him coldly. "D'ya think towin' this truck's gonna be free? Or the gas haulin' yer dumb butt aroun' while yer truck's gettin' fixed is gonna be free?"

"I'll pay," Davis said.

The ol' man huffed. "Boy, yer food ain't free, yer room ain't free, an' this 'ere lady's fence wasn't free, neither."

"Yessir," Davis replied though every thang in 'em wanted ta fight. He could pay for all of it. An' the fence had already been dang near rotten ta begin with. Why should he fix one part if...

"Jus' that part, right?" Davis asked with a point to where the truck shattered the wood into splinters.

"Naw," the old man shook his head.

Post hole digger slid out the back of the truck, along with ten four-by-fours he'd rustled up from behind the shed earlier that mornin'.

22

"Yer gonna work like I'm standin' here. An' if she tells me otherwise, an' she will, you'll be workin' til *I* get tar'd, understand?"

Davis sighed. "Yessir,"

"Best get goin', an' be thankful she didn't call the law on ya this mornin'."

"The law? Why?" Davis replied, tryin' to cover his tail.

The ol' man scowled.

"I've lived 'ere my whole life, turd. An' she's lived 'ere all that an' some. Cain't count on one hand how many deer I've seen crossin' 67 at the bend." He winked with a click sound. "You didn't fool not a soul with tha' nonsense. Now get ta work."

Davis wasn't sure how much time passed, but it never took too long before the Gulf heat spread like a wet blanket of fire an' he's sweatin' from more places than he could count. So much for spring, he thought. Tall Pin Oaks gave a lil' shade here an' there, but even the shade didn't do too much if there wasn't a good breeze ta go with it. He could always tell when it was gonna be a crazy hot one if the cicadas started chirpin' by mid-mornin'. On those days even a good air conditioner could only take the edge off, an' by the looks of the old lady's house he doubted she even had one.

Five mounds of red-orange clay lay heaped in small piles where he'd dug the holes and set the posts, jus' like his old man had shown him a couple summers back. They's always doin' lil' jobs here an' there for extra cash in the fall before Turkey-day. The old man had said it was so Davis could build up them noodle-arms durin' football season before baseball season, but Davis knew he liked the help. Even though they worked mostly in silence or with a radio station blasting classic rock or country, Davis had liked the time together, too. When the pay came, Davis sat shocked when the old man split the profit fifty-fifty. That'd been the first summer he'd felt like a man. He'd saved all his money up that summer to buy the Green Goblin. Now, as he glanced at it again, an' then back to the tools in his hands, he felt an odd connection, almost deja vu like.

"Might fix a fence better 'an you can drive, Davy," a sweet voice said, suddenly behind him.

Davis leapt so fast outta his memory he nearly dropped the post hole digger. He turned to see the tall, tanned girl leanin' with her shoulder against the oak. She shoved a handful of sunflower seeds in her mouth and jammed the bag in the only back pocket her cut-off jean shorts had. Sandy blonde hair pulled back in a ponytail, curly at the tips. Most of it lay hidden under an old Harrison High baseball cap. Freckles danced under dangerous blue eyes. Sleeveless button-up shirt all baby blue plaid. She's every bit as gorgeous as somethin' outta movie. He tried not to gawk at her.

"Don't remember me, do ya?"

"I…," he started until he realized he was 'bout to answer "…could never forget meetin' you" then stopped himself an' just choked on his spit.

"Yeah," she shook her head, obviously either ignorin' his stammerin' or oblivious to his gawkin'. "You's a bit young las' time we saw one another."

She couldn't be too much older than him, could she?

"Heck, you's prob'ly six 'er seven, I suppose."

How old was she?

"I'm Allie," she said, extending her hand with a smile that'd put the sun outta business.

24

"You went ta Harrison?" He nodded toward her hat with a flick-of-a-point before he slid his hat off and brushed the sweat on his forehead away with his sleeve.

She stalled, still perplexed by somethin', as if she'd asked him a question an' he hadn't answered. Finally, she nodded.

"Yep, well, three years, anyhow."

"Oh, where'd ya go after?"

"I didn't. Got my GED. Had to, uh, drop out my senior year."

"Happens," Davis shrugged, tryin' to gather somethin' after gawkin' for so long. "Big baseball fan?"

"Used ta be. Ain't been to a game in, well, ten years."

"Ten?" *How old are ya*, he wanted to ask, but knew better.

"Do you play?" she asked.

"Yeah, an' football, too," he said.

She nodded with a smirk that said somethin', almost like she already knew.

"Well, it's nice talkin' with ya, Davy."

"Yes ma'am," he said. "I shouldn't be but another hour er so," he said.

She shrugged, as if the fence didn't matter to her. "Looks good though."

He spun around an' tried not to watch her sway away. It was easily one o' the hardest things he'd ever done. If she hadn't seen a game in ten years, an' the las' time she saw him he'd been six, *and* she hadn't finished her las' year of school, that'd put her at 'round twenty-six 'er so, he counted in his head as he finished punching the clay down around the last post.

Davis wasn't sure what she did for a livin', but if she wasn't modelin' somethin' she's surely sittin' on easily the best kept secret this side a Crawtaters. Who would've thought *that* could've stepped outta the old house? He took a deep steadying breath before he slid the first Folgers can toward the end of his tailgate an' snatched up his hammer. It was time to move on to the planks. And with any luck he might finish before lunch.

4

UNCUT

SUNDAY

Eggs slid from the iron skillet onto the plate to join the bacon and toast. There were a lot of things Liam wasn't sure about, an' how the girl might react to wakin' up in a stranger's house was at the top of his list. Right next to why she'd been dressed in one of his shirts an' layin' in his bed. He'd slept on the couch, but he wasn't too sure foldin' the sheets up and puttin' the pillow away was such a good idea after all. *Maybe she'd have felt a lot better seein' where he'd slept,* he wondered an hour or so too late.

He'd need more than the deep breath he took, but he took it all the same.

"Mornin'," he said as nicely as he could, tryin' not to spook her.

He failed. The small girl flailed back like a startled cat, an' he's half worried she might pounce like one, too. Every curse he'd ever heard poured from her beautiful mouth an' left him speechless. He'd known friends who'd joined the military an' returned to visit who'd taken up a lot of

27

profanity, an' even they didn't spit it every other word. He sat the tray down on the nightstand an' lifted his hands defensively, steppin' away like she's a rabid critter. In the mix of things, Liam caught a few questions and tried to answer 'em when she'd take a breath.

"I-I'm Liam King," he started.

"You're at my house in Harrison an', uh, I-I found you on the side of the road when I's walkin' home las' night."

"No, ma'am! I didn't do...*we*...didn't do nothin'! I swear!"

"No ma'am! I don't know where yer clothes are."

"I saw the car...," he tried to explain, but she interrupted him, again.

"Tha's *my* shirt. No ma'am, you don't need ta give it back."

"No ma'am, I don't know where yer stuff is."

"No ma'am, I don't know 'em. Didn't even see 'em. I-I saw the car..."

"No ma'am, they didn't. I didn't talk to 'em. They jus' sorta tossed ya out on the road." "No ma'am. They must've kept yer thangs."

"Yes ma'am, I'm serious!"

"Yes ma'am, I always talk like this."

"I-I jus' call ladies, ma'am. That's how I's raised."

"Harrison...Mississippi."

"This 'ere's breakfast. I-I made it fer you...well, fer *us*. I ate mine. I figured you'd be hungry an' I didn't want ya to have nothin' if you woke an' I wasn't here. I'm sorry, I should've waited. I jus'..."

"No ma'am, I's 'bout ta leave fer church."

"Church," he said, again.

"No ma'am, I ain't kiddin'."

"Well, I guess I figured I ain't got a lot you'd probably wanna steal...," he chuckled a little. *Gettin' robbed by a hundred-*

pound girl dang near barefoot an' with no purse, money, car, or phone didn't seem to worry him much, he wanted to reply, but didn't.

She finally stopped yellin' and Liam had a second to breathe. It'd only been half a minute, but he felt like he'd jus' got done runnin' from one o' Mr. Gary's huntin' dogs. It was then he noticed her eyes scannin' him like an x-ray, studyin' him. From his khakis to his button-up shirt, an' even the bible near the door.

"Church, huh?" she asked, calmly.

She slid from her knees on the bed down to the edge and looked at the plate.

"Here," he rushed. "You can come an' sit at the table, if ya like."

"Got any thang ta drink up in 'ere?" she asked.

"Uh, yes ma'am. I got O.J., water, uh, some milk, an' pickle juice it looks like," he laughed.

"So, when we bouncin'?" she asked.

"Bouncin'?"

"Leavin'!" she said, startin' to sound frustrated, again.

"Oh, uh, for what?"

"Church! You said you's goin' ta church. When we leavin'?"

"We? Oh, uh, you ain't gotta come if…"

Pssh! "Nigga, you ain't leavin' me here! Ain't you never seen a scary movie? An' we in Mississippi? Naw! I'm comin' wit' you! You stuck now! You done guardian angeled yo-self."

Liam took a deep breath, tryin' to steady his nerves.

"My mom might have something that'd fit ya, but she's a bit taller than you. She wouldn't mind."

The girl looked down to the long button-up-shirt-turned-skirt an' shrugged.

"I thought you said this's yer place?" she asked. "Why you got yo momma's clothes? Wait! You talkin' 'bout yo baby momma? 'Cause I ain't finna wear some..."

"No ma'am. It ain't like that. I meant *my* momma. They're gone. They live somewhere else. I'm here while they're away."

"By yourself?"

"Yes ma'am!"

"You stay sayin' that, huh?"

"Suppose so."

"An' you cooked this?" she asked.

Liam nodded.

"An' they ain't comin' back anytime soon?"

"Not for at least a year, I reckon."

"You what?"

He smiled. "No ma'am. They're not comin' back anytime soon."

"So you stay in this big house rent free? An' you ain't got no baby momma?"

"No ma'am, I still gotta pay bills an'...*what?* No."

"This a good ride. You straight. An' yo girl ain't gonna be mad you got some candy in yo bed?"

Liam shook his head and tried not to laugh.

"No ma'am. I, uh, I ain't gotta girl." He thumbed over his shoulder. "I slept on the couch. I-I didn't sleep in the bed..."

Mmm-hmm. A smirk crawled on her face, one Liam knew meant she was at least a little relieved. But he could see a hidden pain there, too, one she'd buried, or maybe she'd gotten use to buryin' deeper with the hopes no one might see it. But Liam saw somethin' there he couldn't explain, an' he wasn't sure she should. At least, not to him. She hadn't panicked about the people in the car. Didn't even try to explain them or ask any more about 'em. Most girls would be in a puddle of tears, but somethin' about her seemed like a wall —a well-guarded wall Liam wasn't sure anyone had ever seen behind.

When abuse becomes a common thing, pain is a familiar face in a room of regret, he'd heard someone say once. As Liam looked again at the *thing* he couldn't explain, he nearly heard his heart crack from the weight. Worse, he felt it. He'd known that weight once an' hid it away too. Hid it so far he'd almost forgotten it somehow. Before he could relive the rush of the memories, her gold-brown eyes stole him back.

"Ohhhh," she said smilin'. "Slept on the couch? An' how'd yo shirt get on me, again?"

"I took it off when I found you an'..."

Mmm-hmm. "Yeah! Right... I forgot we's goin' ta church." She winked.

We, he heard her say, again. How was he gonna explain this?

~*~

It was a cute sundress, but longer than mid-thigh on her short frame. All his momma's dresses had a tie 'round the midsection. Jus' another one of them things Liam never noticed when he's younger, but felt a lil' more thankful for now. His Gran would'a said she's skinnier than a dad-gummed soap bubble, but Liam thought it looked good 'nough.

Jewel did, too. Whenever she stood still for any length of time she swayed back and forth an' slid her hands down it an' watched it wrap around her. He'd seen the lil' girls at Sunday school do the same, an' thought it was cute. He'd never seen a woman do it.

Paige and Katy wove around the masses like they usually did until they caught sight of her, then slowed and pretended not to notice. Their faces looked like someone stole the light from the sun. *Maybe this wasn't such a bad idea after all?* On the other side of the room, Cora Lynn walked with Travis an' Mr. Montgomery, both of 'em wavin' like there's nothin' different in the world. Liam breathed a lot easier when the old timer flashed one of his grins. He wasn't sure why, it always meant trouble or orneriness.

If Jewel noticed, he couldn't tell.

"Hi," Cora Lynn said.

"Ms. Jewel, this's Ms. Cora Lynn. She's a friend o' mine. An' this's Travis,"

"Liam's *best* friend," Travis added without looking at her. Likely scannin' to find Ms. Nancy, Liam knew.

"My *best* friend," Liam corrected.

Travis nodded approvingly.

"An' this is Mr. Montgomery."

"Ms. Jewel. Well, if yer name doesn't fit ya darlin'. You've got to be the purdiest thing this ol' man has seen in ages," he said with a wink.

Jewel cocked her head and looked at him. "You blind, huh?"

Liam snickered. Cora Lynn glanced back and forth between everyone, confused.

Mr. Montgomery grinned. "I am now, sunshine."

"Oh, he's a playa. Monte, you a playa. Okay!" She shoved his shoulder. "I see you. You betta get on before you get kicked outta church."

After Mr. Montgomery, Jewel started to come out of her shell a bit. Maybe a lil' too much. She put on the church face an' somehow managed not to spit a single curse word, which amazed Liam more than anything after their introduction. Not that he could blame her.

"You know, Mississippi ain't all white folks an' KKK like they make it sound," she said a lil' too loudly.

"Yeah, we try...," Liam replied with a smirk. "We still got better fried chicken down here though..."

"Oh, he got jokes," she said. "Liam King got jokes y'all! Ha!"

"Liam," a familiar voice stole the moment. Pastor Sam extended his hand.

"Mornin', Pastor. This 'ere's Ms. Jewel. She's visitin' today all the way from Indiana."

"Indiana?" he echoed with a nod. "A Hoosier."

"Uh-huh," she replied.

"An' how'd you find us today all the way out in the middle o' nowhere?"

For some reason the room got really hot to Liam. *Why was he sweatin'?*

"Liam said he's comin'...so he invited me."

"Well good. Good. An' how do you two know one another? Meet at the park?"

Liam's throat knotted up like a lump, risin'.

"The park?" Jewel asked. "Naw, Liam..."

"No, Sir. We met las' night," he interrupted. "So, I asked if she'd like to come this mornin' an' here we are." He could tell she didn't like that he'd cut her off, but it jus' sorta blurted out. *Why am I so scared,* he wondered? He hadn't done anything wrong, had he?

Pastor Sam nodded slowly. "Okay. Well, it's nice meetin' you, Ms. Jewel. We got a nice young ladies' group out that-a-ways. Liam, you can show her before yer class, cain't ya?"

"Uh, Yessir."

The look on Jewel's face told Liam he'd need to explain a few things an' quick. She looked a few seconds away from a dozen questions.

"A *ladies'* group?"

Liam wanted to shush her. Since when did everyone else seem so quiet? For such a small thing, she had a set of lungs on her.

"It's a...so, uh, before church we split into groups an' have lil' classes we go to...ta get ta know folks an' talk an' study. Then, we come back in the sanctuary an' have church."

"Like church-church?"

"Yes 'am, but *after* the smaller groups."

"An' you gonna be there?"

"Fer church-church, but not the ladies' group."

She started to shake her head.

"They won't bite ya, Ms. Jewel," he said as comforting as he could muster. He even touched her shoulder.

"I don't know," she said, eyeing the door.

"Jus' give it a look, first. If ya don't wanna, don't. I'll stay with ya."

"You ain't teachin'?"

Liam shrugged. "Not if you want me ta stay with ya."

"You won't get in trouble or..."

He shrugged again. "I can pass my lesson on to someone else. Jesus has been doin' this thang long before Liam King, an' I reckon he'll be doin' it long after, too."

"You 'bout fried," she said, and Liam could see it there again behind the wall. Relief.

How many people had left her, he wondered?

"I'd a left ya in the dark las' night if I's gonna leave ya, Ms. Jewel."

Something happened at that moment, an' Jewel knew it too.

"Okay," she breathed, then cleared her throat with a nod. "Okay," she said, again. A lil' tougher, as if he hadn't heard it the first time. "Imma be a *lady*, I guess. You get on an' teach yo Man's class."

5

NEVER LEAVIN'

SUNDAY

"Mornin', Darlin'…"

"Hey, Hunnnney…"

"Well, ain't you a peach?"

Were they serious? It was somethin' outta movie, an' all their accents seemed to stretch even the smallest words 'bout five times longer than they needed to, like they's mouth full of food or somethin'.

But at least they were happy an' smilin'. They must've been the smilin'est people Jewel'd ever saw in her life. She hadn't encountered many people who smiled at her all the time, an' only those were boys, and they had another look in their eyes when they did.

The thought brought a flash of the memory, but it was still blurry. Hands. Lots of hands.

Her skin crawled an' the small shiver hadn't been missed by one of the other ladies.

"We *do* keep that AC goin', huh?" the old woman said. "Here, you can use my lil' jacket an' cover yer legs, sweetheart."

"Come on in an' 'ave a seat, Sugar," another lady said.

"A-right, mommas!" another voice interrupted. She was a young woman. Well, young*er*. She's pro'lly in her thirties, an' fit too, but she had a look to her said she had a lil' street. Jewel felt like they knew one another from somewhere.

"Y'all let this girl alone. She jus' need a seat an' some juice." She winked at Jewel. "We got orange, grape, an' I ain't even sure what that is...yeah, we ain't touchin' 'at." She snarled.

Jewel smirked. *Shay*, she realized. The woman reminded her of an older, prettier Shayla.

She didn't ask any of the normal questions everyone else did, like she didn't 'ave time to or somethin'. "I'm Tamra Winslow. I got two girls off in classes, an' my husband's 'roun' 'ere teachin' in one o' these classes." Her accent sounded like all the others, but not as slow an' thick. An' she talked with her hands an' her neck, jus' like Shayla.

"I'm Jewel. I'm from Indy. Jus' visitin' durin' break."

"Okay, Jewel from Indy. What you doin' for lunch?"

"I...uh...I dunno."

Tamra made a face, all scrunched up like she's gonna ask *'Girl, how you don't know?'*

"Well, we eatin' at Fancy's then. I hope you hungry."

Jewel wanted to say she wasn't sure, or explain a lil' more about Liam an' not knowing if she should, but all the words jumbled in her throat. Tamra hadn't *asked* anything. Jewel'd been told! 'Bout that time, a cute-lookin' blonde woman with her hair all up an' a sundress like Jewel's came in, hugged Tamra an' pointed at Jewel. She sounded southern an' sweet, but her words weren't extra long like the others.

"This your sister?"

"Girl, shut up!" Tamra said with a laugh. "You lyin' in church too, thinkin' I look young an' beautiful like this thang."

She shrugged. Tamra shook her head.

"Jewel, this sweet-talkin' woman is one of our pastors' wives, Angelina."

"They call me Angel," she said, extending her hand.

"Yeah, but *I* ain't gonna lie in church," Tamra said, smirking.

"Oh, okay," Angel said. When she raised her hand to her mouth to pretend she was shocked, Tamra leaned away like she's dodgin' a slap.

"*One* of the pastor's wives?" Jewel echoed. "How many wives he got?"

Tamra almost fell on the floor laughin'.

"I didn't even think 'bout how that sounded," she said in-between breaths.

"Imma tell Chris that one!" Angel said as she continued huggin' a few of the women.

"You better ask'm first, girl!" Tamra replied. "Jus' ta make sure."

"Girl, he ain't got enough money for more than me," Angel added. "What you doin' for lunch?"

"It's Sunday, girl. Fancy's."

"You stay at Fancy's on Sundays."

"Girl, we eat out once a week. I ain't chancin' my money on trash. Besides, you tell me who has better food for a better price an' free tea? I'll wait."

"Ever had Fancy's, Ms. Jewel?" Angel asked.

"I haven't really eaten anywhere...other than Liam's."

"Liam's?" Angel echoed.

"Liam King?" Tamra asked.

"Yeah, he made me breakfast this mornin', an' I had a burger down on the beach yesterday, but it was trash. Other than that, I ain't had much since the bus left Indy. But, by the sound o' thangs Imma have diabetes 'fore I leave this place."

Tamra smiled. "Tha's 'bout right."

"You ate breakfast with Liam this mornin'?" Angel asked, still confused. "That's awfully sweet of him."

"He's a good cook," Jewel said.

"He brought biscuits when we had'm over last," Tamra said, noddin'. "An' they weren't the frozen ones. Scratch, too. He's handy in the kitchen. Almost took the shine off my chicken."

Angel raised an eyebrow.

"Girl, I said *almost*. Don't light a fuse. Start your class, I'm gettin' hungry."

All the women stopped huggin' an' sat down, until only Angel stood. She unzipped her bible case and opened it to the lil' ribbon page, then flipped her notebook open beside it.

"A'ight y'all. Before we get started Tamra volunteered to lead us in prayer."

"I did?"

Angel glared at her.

"I *did*...," she said soundin' all convinced. "Yeah, you know I did girls. *Okay*."

The women laughed along as if they's used to them actin' a fool. All the women took hands 'round the table. Tamra grabbed Jewel's without a second thought.

"Let's pray like we need to, ladies," she said. "'Cause we do."

Jewel felt weird holdin' hands an' for some reason the chill of the room was gone suddenly, replaced by somethin'

39

else —was it worry? It was like she was steppin' out into the middle o' somethin' an' now she could be seen. That's what it was, she realized. Exposed. She felt open, like that one roach in the middle o' the kitchen floor when the lights turned on. All the other ones skittered away, an' hid under the dishes or behind the trash, but there's always tha' one jus' froze in the middle like no one could see it. She imagined it like a lil' kid an' how they's always thankin' they could jus' close their eyes durin' hide an' seek an' the seeker wouldn't find 'em.

Only everyone *could* see Jewel.

But not jus' everyone else.

Him.

The one she'd been hidin' from, or at least she thought she had.

She pinched her eyes shut as Tamra started. That's what they all did in the movies.

Suddenly, Jewel was *there* again. White sand under her toes. Music bumpin' all 'round. A crowd of black men an' women with they phones out makin' videos an' snappin'. They's dancin'. Cars sat revvin' they engines. One Escalade had boxes from top to bottom. Bass was hittin' so hard her eyes couldn't see straight. She saw the one guy, the small one. Everyone had drinks in they hands. He was talkin' 'bout somethin', but she couldn't hear it all, an' she couldn't remember. Two more drinks by sunset. The beach was so beautiful. It was the first time she'd ever seen a beach. In Indy all they had was big lakes, an' she hadn't even been to see them. How could a day so beautiful end so horribly?

The memory slid away with the first tear down her cheek, then another.

She felt the hands again, then slid away. Her eyes flicked open, lights spinning. A dark figure loomed over her with a starlit sky above. It was Liam. Another tear.

"Jesus," he kept sayin' like he's scared.

Why's he so scared, she wondered? He didn't even know her? Why'd he even care? Why'd he even stop? Back home people jus' minds they own bidness.

But not Liam. *'I ain't leavin' ya,'* he'd said with his country twang. An' there's somethin' there in his eyes tol' 'er she could trust him. She'd never admit it to anyone, but she could feel it like the sound of thunder when you don't see the lightnin', but how you *know* one ain't without the other.

Another tear. She couldn't wipe 'em, her hands held by the others.

Why'd he do that? Why'd he dress her in his shirt? Why'd he take her home? An' he didn't even have a car. He hadn't tossed her in the backseat, he'd carried her sweaty nasty self. Who knows what they did before they dumped her? An' he carried her all nasty? Who does that? Who touches somethin' like that, doesn't call the cops, an' makes breakfast? Who invites somebody in they house an' ain't scared o' gettin' stabbed in they sleep? Then, after all dat, takes 'em to they church? She shook her head, frustrated an' confused, but not by him. She's mad, but not at Liam.

Girl, you *so* dumb!

Naw, you's loved, a second voice argued. It sounded like Tamra's, but she's still prayin'.

Loved? Why? What you done to be loved? The voice she'd heard her whole life fought back, remindin' her what all the other people in her life had said an' done since her momma left her with her boyfriend 'cause her new daddy didn't want her mixin' wit all his kids an' they mommas.

41

Since when you gotta do somethin' to be loved? Tamra's voice asked in her mind. She felt it askin' her like she'd been asked to eat lunch all over again. It wasn't askin' her, it was tellin' her! *Why you gotta earn my love?*

My? Jewels wondered a moment, but the answer was already there before she could finish askin'. Another tear fell, and another.

She sniffled. It was *Him*. Then, Tamra's words –her real words– settled in her ears.

"Jesus, we thank you for your love, your mercy, grace, an' for forgivin' our sins. Help us to hear you today. In your sweet name, Amen." Tamra opened her eyes and glanced at Jewel confused. All the women 'roun' the table said 'Amen', but Jewel didn't care when their eyes turned to the scene, one by one. She could only stare back at Tamra.

"I want that," Jewel said. Her shoulders shook as more tears fell from somewhere she'd buried away sleepin' on strangers couches in houses with hands, in the backseats of cars with hands, an' under the smells an' sounds echoin' in her mind. She didn't want that life anymore. She didn't want Indy. She didn't want to be *her*.

"You wanna know Jesus, girl?" Tamra asked. She yanked her into a hug, squeezin' her tighter an' closer than Jewels could ever remember someone holdin' her.

She felt it, the lightning with the thunder –the feelin' of the love with the thought of it.

"I heard of 'em. I ain't never known him," Jewel cried.

"It's aight," Tamra whispered as Jewels continued to cry on her shoulder. "He's known you. He sees that heart an' he's ready to work on it. Come on," she said. "You jus' tell'm how you feel."

~*~

Liam stood by the door when the class was dismissed. When Jewel didn't rush out, he stuck his head in an' his expression took Angel by surprise.

"Hey you," she said. After a brief hug, she smiled, calmin' his nerves. "You aight?"

"Yeah, you seen…"

"Tamra has her," Angel said, tryin' to hide a grin.

He tried to hide his relief. *What would she do*, he wondered? *Walk away? To where? After all, who'd she know?*

"What?" Liam asked when her grin continued to linger.

"Nutin'," she replied, rocking her shoulder into him. She was almost ten years older, but they'd known one another their entire lives.

When Liam didn't press the conversation, Angel's orneriness only increased.

"She's a lil' head-turner, Mr. King. Are there a few lil' gals 'round 'ere gonna need some counselin' soon?"

Liam shook his head. Jus' like the older sister he never wanted.

"She's a lil' rough 'round the edges, but…," she teased.

"Oh, knock it off!" he replied. "Don't make me tell Chris about the ridin' mower water hose incident."

"I thought it'd go over it!" she whisper-growled. "Okay, okay!"

"Why's she with Tamra? Before class she seemed as shaky as a leaf. I's expectin' my class door to fly open any secon'."

They entered the assembly hall an' his eyes instantly found her. Not because she stood out, but because of where she stood. Near the front. On the platform. In white robes.

His jaw dropped.

"Yeah, so...uh...that happened," Angel added with a surprise giggle.

"Man, y'all's ladies' group is puttin' my group to shame, sis."

"What can I say, when ya got it, ya got it."

Liam shook his head, though his eyes couldn't linger from the sight of her. When Jewel finally found him, she smiled, still crying, and shrugged. He shrugged back with a smile.

"Oh, an' we're all eatin' at Fancy's apparently," Angel added.

"Tamra, huh?"

"Yessir."

6

THE OPPOSITE OF NOTHIN'

SUNDAY EVENIN'

A lot of families from church went to Fancy's. Liam had noticed before, but somehow forgotten. That is, until more than one set of eyes stared at him showin' Jewel through the slang menu an' then up and down the buffet line. Northerners didn't have thangs like pickled okra, fried okra, fried onions an' taters, red beans an' rice, or peach cobbler.

"What y'all eat?" he joked.

"Not this," she replied with a snarl at the liver an' onions. "They serious, huh?"

He laughed.

"What's a *po*-boy?"

"Bes' sammich you ever had, girl," Tamra's husband, Terry, replied as he slid past her in the line.

"Shrimp, lettuce, mayo," Liam started.

"Girl," Tamra interjected, shakin' her head. "Don't listen ta them when it comes ta food. We don't come to Fancy's for no sammich, or whatever *that* is," she snarled, pointing at something. She shook her head. "Naw, we come for the fried chicken, mashed potatoes an' gravy…"

"Homemade biscuits…," Angel added.

"Mac an' cheese," Tamra said.

They wiggled their way between Jewel and Liam an' shewed him toward the other men.

"Honey butter…," Angel continued.

"Cajun rice," Tamra added

"Oh, girl, I forgot the rice."

Tamra stopped and stared at Angel like she's crazy an' they both watched her shuffle back down the buffet line an' squeeze in-between a couple to hurriedly get a scoop.

"'Scuse me, darlin'," she said sweetly. "Got an' emergency here. Gotta get some o' this before Jesus comes back."

Chris shook his head at his wife. Everyone else laughed.

"That's aight, bro," Terry consoled him. "Tamra will straight up stand at the empty fried chicken pan an' hold up the whole line without a word 'til they hurry up an' bring it from the drive-thru."

"When Angel was pregnant she cried one time when they didn't have honey butter."

"Y'all shut up 'bout my butter. Honey butter'll be in heaven, y'all," Angel chimed in, suddenly there. Somehow she had another plate, this one with three biscuits an' peach cobbler.

"Dang girl, d'you eat already?" Terry asked, wide-eyed.

She scoffed. "No. I'm stockin' up!"

"They crazy," Jewel whispered, snatching Liam from the scene. He could only nod.

"Yeah, we can't pick family," he said, shakin' his head.

"Family?"

"*Church* family," he replied. "We've all known one another since...forever. My folks used to be the pastors here before I graduated."

"Mus' be nice, livin' in a small place, surrounded by people like this all the time." Her eyes seemed sad for a secon', like a memory snatchin' her back to Indy.

"Yeah, but it ain't always like this," he admitted. "Life ain't perfect anywhere, I reckon."

"It ain't? I mean, I know life ain't perfect, but they ain't like this all the time?"

He knew what she meant an' he could almost feel that desire to find somethin' fake in it all, some sort of peace tha' came when somethin' too good had a flaw. *Why'd that always seem to make things more comfortable*, he wondered? Folks always looked for that when it came to church –somethin' fake. When it came to church-folks everyone played the detective huntin' for any lil' clue to find a fraud. Liam almost snickered, rememberin' Mr. Montgomery's words a long time ago. *Church is like a gym, son*, he'd said. *It ain't only for the skinny, muscular folks*. Jewel's question still lingered there, hoping for an answer to ease her mind one way or another. Which way? He wasn't sure, exactly.

"Angel an' Tamra? Yeah. They're *always* crazy.

"I heard dat," Tamra said without lookin'. "Don't think I'm leavin' you any spicy legs, Mr. King."

"That's not what Jesus would do," Terry interjected.

"You wrong for that, Sir," she said. "Bes' mind your business, or tha' chicken ain't gonna be the only salty thing you're gonna have on your hands."

"Woman, he's a man! He ain't afraid o' you!" Chris said as he passed by. He patted Terry on the back. "I got you, bro!"

"Shut up, dude!" Terry said, quickly. "I ain't tryin' ta sleep on the couch."

"Don't you laugh either, or I ain't even leavin' you the crunchies at the bottom of the pan," Terry threatened, holdin' the tongs toward Liam with a snap.

~*~

After lunch, the girls announced they were takin' Jewel on a walk down the road to the little shops behind Marco's, the ice cream place on the corner. Everything could change in Harrison, but there were a few things never did. They'd grown up there, on that corner. Almos' every summer memory he'd had as a kid had been under the covered porches at one of those picnic tables durin' the heat of an unforgivin' day, or under the fat strings of lights passin' in-between poles cemented in the tires scattered around the lot. Eatin' at Fancy's after church or Uncle Bob's Barbecue. The quick stops to get gas an' grab the best cold Barq's root beer from the cooler in the back of Nic Nac Grocery.

As Liam watched Jewel glance at him over her shoulder to check an' make sure he still wasn't leavin', he couldn't help but wonder if she'd had any of those sorts of thangs back in Indy. He hadn't been many places 'round the states. In truth, it was embarassin' how lil' he'd traveled in his own country compared to where he'd been with his folks overseas on mission trips with the church. He spoke Spanish pretty good after three or four trips to Mexico, an' even a little French creole from the times they'd gone to Haiti. 'Course he'd been to the other places along the gulf, too –

Lousy-ana, 'Bama, an' Southeastern California, also known as Florida. But never anywhere up north like Indy.

Liam walked with Terry an' Chris back to the church to grab the trucks. With the Sunday lunch rush over, the parkin' would be a lil' better, but not much.

"I know you stay walkin', man," Terry said. "An' y'all didn't drive in *her* car this mornin' to church," he added. "An' I know you're up with the sun. So, how'd you make breakfas' for her this mornin'?"

Chris' eyebrows lifted though his face was in his phone.

"I don't think she has a car," Liam replied. "At least, not here. Maybe back in Indy."

"Good answer, good answer," Chris said.

"You didn't answer my question, bruh," Terry said.

"Also true, true." Chris nodded, still looking at his phone.

"She stayed at your place las' night, huh?" he asked boldly.

"Yeah," Liam said. He knew how it sounded.

"Okay, okay. Story time," Chris added.

"Dude, we know you," Terry said with a sigh. "I know you ain't like *dat*. But tha's how it looks, an' folks all about how thangs look. Some out to protec' you," he said, pointin' between the two of them, "but others wanna hear the juice. An' if they don't hear it, their imagination'll help 'em make it up."

"Yeah, an' your defense better be better than mine is righ' now 'cause I'm getting' killed!" Chris added. "Three touchdowns! Really?"

"Touchdowns?" Liam echoed. "It's not football season."

"Online Madden season," Terry replied. "He stays football."

49

"Stays losin', too!" Chris mumbled.

"Who chooses the Jags, bruh?" Terry said, shakin' his head.

"I got las' pick!"

"You showed up late...anyhow...Chris is right. You cain't show up late to the table an' have a bad defense." He glanced at Liam waitin' for him to explain the whole story, but Liam knew he shouldn't.

"I should talk with her, first," he said. "She might not feel right if I told anybody her situation, you know?"

"Hey, you right! I respect that," Terry replied. "You a knight, my-man. No doubts from me...but I *do* need to know what's the plan?"

Liam couldn't respond. What *could* he say? He hadn't really had the time to think about any of it. Where they could sleep had been easy an' it'd be even easier once he cleared out the guest room. Of course, how others might view it all lingered aroun' his mind. Liam had hoped his character meant somethin', but he couldn't doubt the truth of Terry's words. Someone somewhere wouldn't be as bold an' curious to get to the truth as Terry an' Chris. What would he do then?

"Have you tol' Pastor Sam?"

"No, not yet."

"Step one," Chris chimed in. "QB needs to know the play, bruh."

"I ain't even really talked to Jewels 'bout any of it, yet. It's been a crazy day."

With all her thangs missin', Liam jus' sort of assumed he'd be buyin' a ticket for her back to Indy sometime tomorrow an' this'd be behind him by the middle of the week.

"She'll probably need a ticket back to Indy," Liam thought out loud.

"You see the look on her face, man?" Terry replied.

Liam had, but as he stared into the doubtful expression of his adopted older church brother he realized he may've missed a thang or two.

"Yeah, she ain't goin' back to Indy," Chris said, still lookin' at his phone. "She's already traded the blue an' white for the black an' gold, babay."

"You better be talkin' 'bout my Golden Eagles, 'cause I know she ain't gonna be no Saints fan."

Chris looked up from his phone slowly, like he'd been punched, then turned it to face Terry. "Looks like dem Cowboys o' yours are losin' to the Jags right now, an' las' I checked my Bulldogs don't wear black an' gold, so..."

"Y'all got issues," Liam said. "You know tha', right?"

"My bad," Terry apologized. Chris slid his phone away.

"It's all true though, buddy. These things can get stupid, an' quick."

"If it's like you said, an' she's not goin' back...," Liam shrugged. What was he supposed to do? Leave her hangin'?

"You know, if you'd take a step in this century an' get at leas' a prepaid phone, things might be easier," Terry said.

Liam nodded. Everyone said the same things every time he had any sort of situation. When the washing machine hose started leaking, the first complaint was his lack of a phone. If he left his bible at church, the only solution was to buy a phone. Liam had learned a very important lesson years ago, one he'd never be able to unlearn. If the whole world is doing somethin' an' you don't...everyone's uncomfortable 'til you join the herd. There's jus' somethin' 'bout bein' the outsider tha' makes the insiders squirm. Liam didn't like makin' others squirm or anything, but he didn't see the need as much. Work had a phone. Church had a phone. His house had a phone an' at least two computers. Everyone else in the world had phones he could use if he needed to. Truth was, he didn't want one. An' there wasn't a day went by, while the whole world looked down, he wasn't lookin' up. *That!* That's what he liked most. An' deep down he knew that's what he'd miss. Lookin' up. Sunlight. Moments. Faces of folks. The smiles on the ol' couples faces walkin' on the beach.

"Yeah, I'm sure me getting' a phone'll fix this whole mess right up," he said with a chuckle. He patted the guys on the shoulders. "You two are the best an' the worst. I'll call Pastor Sam an' I'll talk with Jewel this evenin' 'bout what she wants ta do. I jus' hope I can help her through whatever it is she's goin' or been through."

"You already did," Terry said, smilin'.

Before Liam could shake the words away, Chris slapped him on the shoulder, noddin'.

"He's righ', man! I don't know what's up, but you *definitely* led her to save her soul this mornin'. That ain't nothin', man. Tha's the opposite of nothin'."

"You doin' righ'," Terry said. "Jus' remember how others can look at thangs, too, is all we're sayin'. Keep folks' mouths on a leash."

"A short leash!" Chris added.

"Pitbull muzzle tha' thang."

7

REMEMBERIN'

SUNDAY EVENIN'

"**M**r. Tommy won't be 'round with the tow truck 'til this evenin'," Ms. Luanne said just before lunchtime.

'I figured,' Davis wanted to reply, but didn't. After workin' hard all mornin' replacin' the fencing down the front of the property, clear from the drive to the brush near the corner, he'd done two fellas' worth of work in half the time. Now, he'd finished the task, an' found himself stuck at the mercy of the old woman who seemed more than eager to keep him busy.

He'd fixed two hurricane shudders 'round back; removed half a dozen rottin' boards from the porch, and started leveling the railing to readjust where it'd been poorly fixed by someone before. Allie came with a pitcher and nodded toward the swing.

"Come have a seat Davy," she said. "Got some tea for ya."

"Luzianne?" he asked, eager to keep any sort of conversation goin'.

"Is there any other kind?"

"I've had worse."

"We don't make nasty stuff 'roun' 'ere," Ms. Luanne added from somewhere in the darkness beyond the screens. "No self-respectin' folks drink jus' any ol' tea."

"I hear folks up north ask if ya want it sweet or *un*sweet." Davis said.

"Savages," Allie shook her head and pretended to be disgusted.

"Downright sinful!" Ms. Luanne hollered from somewhere beyond. "An' folks say they got better schoolin' up there. *Pssh!* Goes ta show you can be smart *an'* still be stupid, I reckon. Your momma was 'bout the only thang the north ever made worth havin.' Tha's why we stole her!" Ms. Luanne added with a cackle. "She's jus' a southerner God had born up there an' brought back to the Promised Land, I suppose."

Davis sat his tea down an' something 'bout the sight of his expression stole Allie's grin.

"Y'all knew my momma?" he asked.

"Course!" Ms. Luanne replied. She couldn't see what Allie could, an' by the look on her face Davis knew Allie wished she could.

"We were all purdy close back then," Allie added in a hurried whisper. "Hey momma, ain't it time for us to get ta Kelli?"

"Why d'you thank I'm gettin' all gussied up?" came a reply. "For my health?"

Ms. Luanne appeared on the front porch wearin' a pair of salmon slacks, loafers, a sky blue shirt, and a hat the size of Harrison.

"Well, you weren't kiddin' 'bout the gussied up, woman!" Allie replied. "You gonna shade 'bout four or five kids under that thang."

With a scowl that made Davis want to hide, Ms. Luanne glared at her. "You don't like my hat or you jus' jealous?"

"I…"

"Too bad!" Ms. Luanne interrupted. "I don't care how hard you try, you can't have it!"

"Dang! Caught me, again." Allie replied.

"Keep it up, I'll make this shoe disappear up your backside, girl!"

"Yes ma'am," Allie said with a grin. She winked at Davis when her mom turned back around with her wallet in her hand. "We ought ta be back in about an hour or so, Davy. If ya need the bathroom it's in the back next to the backdoor, by the laundry room. If ya leave before then, don't worry 'bout nothin'. We get 'bout as many visitors up 'ere as the beach at Christmastime. If somebody else wrecks in my ditch you jus' have 'em start plowin' my vegetable garden now, ya hear?"

"Yes ma'am," Davis replied with a smirk. "Thanks for the tea."

He walked down to the tailgate of his pickup an' grabbed the screw gun an' the other coffee can with screws when the sound of the tires crackled on the gravel from the covered garage in back. Seemed silly watchin' Ms. Luanne drive such a thing, peekin' over the steerin' wheel big hat an' all, but nothin' 'bout the old woman *hadn't* been so far. Allie waved when they pulled out and Davis sighed.

Did she know how beautiful she was, he wondered as she swiped a few loose strands of hair from her eyes? He shook his head. *'Downrigh' shame,'* he heard one of his buddies say as if they'd been standin' next to him. After a few seconds the thought continued. Why hadn't they been there next to him like a good friend ought to?

Hell, why hadn't they even called him since he left the house las' night? They probably saw the truck in the ditch.

The thought stuck with'm an' gnawed at him 'til the old man came unexpectedly an hour later. Davis started to carry the supplies to the truck, but he waved him back.

"Better off leavin' 'em so we ain't gotta haul 'em back out again."

"Again? Truck's gettin' towed this evenin' is what Ms. Luanne said you'd said."

"Yep, but tha' don't mean we're done workin' 'round here, bud."

Davis put his hands on his hips and half-scoffed, trying to find the right words, but the ol' man kept talkin'.

"I got my schedule switched today. I've got the next two days off."

He scratched his head with the bill of his hat, then slid it back on. "Figured with it bein' Spring Break an' whatnot, an' since you ain't gotta work or anywhere to go anyhow, may as well do a lil' more hard work for a lady who needs it."

Davis could say no, but he knew what that meant. All day sittin' 'round the house doin' nothing, an' with nowhere to go versus the chance of seein' Allie at least a few more times. And with the thought of his 'friends', an' the likelihood of them bein' as scarce as a dog that'd gotten in the trash at the sight o' his truck in the ditch, Davis knew he really only had one choice.

He nodded.

"Tell ya what," the old man said once they hopped in the truck. "I'll sweeten the deal. Every day we work, we'll head over to Marco's an' grab dinner. That'll be yer paycheck."

Hmm, Davis sounded. "Seasoned fries *and* butterscotch shakes, an' you got yerself a deal."

"Tryin' ta break me? I ain't made-a-money!" he said with a grin. "Aight...tough bargain."

They shook on it.

It was the first time he could remember seein' the old man smile in a long time, an' Davis couldn't shake the thought of why it was he'd never cared to notice he hadn't before then.

~*~

They slipped in town an' grabbed some groceries, then stopped by the Farmer's market before they circled back to the house for the evenin' to watch the Sea Wolves. Davis felt like they'd forgotten something the entire trip, but didn't notice 'til they loaded the groceries in the fridge. All the beer was gone. *They'd forgot the necessities?* Not only had they forgotten 'em, but now that he thought about it, they'd passed by the aisle altogether. Hadn't even walked down it. Of course, it was across from the bacon and meats, which is understandable, but still...they never forgot 'the juice'. Since he'd been as young as he could remember they'd always kept beer in the fridge, an' he'd never been held back from havin' one whenever he wanted.

It was one of the first things his friends were always amazed by whenever they stopped by —how cool and easy goin' his old man was 'bout those sorts of things. 'Course, Davis knew it was likely a good reason why he hadn't done much drinkin' outside o' the house, either. Parties weren't as 'sneaky' an' wild to him. He could jus' sit at home and drink whenever he wanted. All the other kids drank like they's thirstin' to death for two or three hours then did a bunch of stupid stuff to tell stories about later. 'Course the other night had been a rare occasion.

But hadn't there been beer in there jus' the other night?

"Knew we forgot somethin'," he said. Davis opened the fridge wider so the ol' man could see from the livin' room chair. "How'd we forget the pee juice?"

The old man waved in reply, dismissin' it. "We'll pick some up later," he said. "Besides, we've got tea, ain't we?"

"Yessir," Davis said. "An' plenty o' ice."

"Suppose I'll let it slide this time then," he said, as if it'd been Davis' fault.

"I…"

"What!" he hollered at the television. Another bad call by the refs. "Don't make me throw my taco burger!" he growled at the TV.

Davis poured two tall glasses of tea an' headed back to the game as another whistle sounded.

"Boy, you'd better get in 'ere 'fore I reach through this TV an' slap this fella! Roughin'? Really? They can fight, ref. He's called an enforcer."

"Maybe they thought it was ballet or somethin'?" Davis said with a twirl.

The ol' man almost choked on his taco burger tryin' not to laugh. By the end of the second period the game was tied, but it was gettin' so late neither one of 'em wanted to stay up anymore. An' with the thought of wakin' early to get back to work at Ms. Luanne's, an' from the beatin' he'd taken from the sun all day, Davis could feel the bed callin' his name. When the ol' man tossed the remote to him, Davis waved him away an' sat up on the couch and turned it off.

"I'm hittin' the hay, too," Davis said.

"Gettin' old, huh?" he chuckled.

It wasn't 'til he turned on his bedside lamp an' kicked the door prop outta the way, Davis caught a glimpse of the cedar chest. He'd slid it out from under the bed and had it opened. He couldn't remember the las' time he'd seen the ol' man touch it, or exactly what was in it. As the door eased closed, he grabbed the empty glasses an' tossed 'em in the cold soapy water sittin' in the sink. It wasn't that the thought wasn't naggin' at him somewhere in the back of his mind, it jus' wasn't overpowerin' the other chant comin' from his muscles and eyes.

Bed! Bed! Bed! No, don't brush yer teeth...y'ain't got time fer that, neither! Bed! Bed!

Davis fought the urge an' brushed his teeth anyway. By the time he laid down, he could already hear the faint snorin' of the ol' man. With the moonlight crashin' through his open blinds, Davis put his hands behind his head an' jus' laid there, thinkin'. It'd been a full day to be sure, but there'd been so many things —comments an' whatnot— naggin' questions at him that he didn't have a clue how to answer. How'd Ms. Luanne an' Allie know him? Not jus' him, he reconsidered, but his whole dad-gummed family even? There were other questions, too, but those were the ones he remembered las' before finally noddin' off to sleep to the sound of the bugs serenadin'.

8

SOMEONE TO WALK WITH

SUNDAY EVENIN'

Liam took her bags an' set them on the table by the door. He'd done it all: opened the door before she got in the truck, took her shoppin' bags, opened the doors to the house, then asked if she wanted some tea. *He stayed doin' the most!*

"So now that ya don't 'ave to eat for two days, an' yer ears done been talked off, I'd understand if ya wanna go off by yourself for a lil' while?" he said.

Jewels jus' stood beside the door starin' at him.

"Sometimes silence is gold, right?"

What'd that even mean? White boys stay sayin' craziness.

She knew she looked fried, but for once she didn't really care. It felt like she'd jus' stepped inside a warm house during winter —when the wind raced over the hill by 10th Street an' hurt her face so bad she couldn't feel it, like all her fingers was numb an' her cheeks was on fire, jus' twitchin' as they thawed. Tha's what it was —she felt like a block o' ice thawin', only sayin' it would-a sounded stupid in Mississippi heat. Even in March. She'd heard they didn't even know what snow was down here.

He gonna thank I done los' my mind!

"I...I don't know what to do," she blurted.

Her mouth snitched on her before she could stop it. Eyes flicked to the old wood floor, to Liam, an' then 'round the house an' all Liam did was slide down into the chair beside the table an' run his hand through his hair. There was somethin' there, again, in his eyes. She'd seen all sorts o' boys eyin' her growin' up. They'd all wanted somethin', an' they all knew how ta act ta get it. They's all actors, jus' playin' 'til what they wanted got laid out in front of 'em an' then they masks chipped off an' they real faces showed tha' smile, like *gotcha.* Jewels ain't been played in years —an' she wouldn't— but these eyes weren't the same.

Liam was in his feelin's, but not *for* her...

He was in his feelin's *over* her.

Those two weren't the same.

Suddenly, she was mad, but deep down she knew it was more like angry-confused.

"Why you muggin' me like dat?"

"I-I...*muggin'*? I-I jus' don't know what to do, either," he replied. "I mean, I dunno what you *need* me ta do. I-I wanna help. Like call the police an' report yer stuff stolen? Or-or buy you a ticket back to Indy? Or..."

Need? I don't need you!

They's there, again. The tears. Snitchin'. A hand covered her mouth an' she tried to wipe them away, but with every hand too many more filled they place, until finally she stumbled back against the door and slid down. She couldn't control them anymore. For years she'd been tough. Before she came to Harrison, she couldn't remember the last time she cried. Now it was like church an' bein' baptized had made her weak or somethin'. Jewels wanted to fall through it, back, away from the past few days, but she didn't want Indy. She'd lived her whole life in Indy, an' if she's real with herself, she didn't like that scene. The danger of 10th an' Washington. She didn't like *that* her, *that* life. The things she'd done to help her momma pay rent. Trap houses. Boys shot walkin' home. An' no matter where she went, she stay seein' people she knew, ones who knew 'bout her.

The closest she got to disappearin' was slappin' the door.

Liam eased to his feet. She wanted to tell'm she wasn't mad, not at him, an' that she's angry, but not at herself. Jus'...every thang. Life. From yesterday to las' night, then today. What was goin' on? Nothin' normal, but every-thang felt right.

Not *right*, she realized.

Fixed.

Made right. Jesus really *had* done somethin'. Jewels felt it. But she couldn't understand it, an' that messed with her head. She needed somethin', but didn't know what. Every time she tried, she couldn't remember the taste-a thangs — the drugs or the drinks.

Liam was there an' she hated him for it. Not *really*, but she did. She glared at him, darin' him to touch her, but then shied away, shakin' her head. She didn't want him to touch her.

Because he shouldn't. Why'd she deserve it? The kindness.

His hands stretched out like she was gonna stab 'em, slow an' easy, but when she didn't, he touched her gingerly until he could finally lift her back up and wrapped his big arms 'round her, smotherin' her into his shirt.

"I'm sorry," he said 'bout a dozen times. She cried an' shook. He carried her to the couch an' sat down, holdin' her like she's a lil' girl with a scraped knee. Even her daddy hadn't done 'at.

Shut yo cryin' up! You bes' dry up 'dem eyes! Don't nobody care nothin' 'bout no bald-headed two-tone girl!

"Don't leave," she heard herself mumble between the tears an' snifflin'.

"I ain't goin' nowhere. You ain't gotta go nowhere. It's okay. Just close yer eyes."

When Jewels woke up, the thin blanket on the back of the couch had been draped over her. Nothin' was quiet in Indy. In Harrison, the silence was so loud she felt scared, like the second in the movie right before the killer jumped out. The sound of her own cryin' annoyed her at first, echoin' off the walls, but now only the rustle of the leaves fumbled in from the screen door in the kitchen where Liam had left it open. She could smell the grill goin', the charcoal and a familiar whiff of hot dogs.

A thick book like a journal lay on the countertop by the door. It was nice, too, all leathery with a buckle. Looked expensive. Bits an' pieces of paper danced out, but a mechanical pencil held the pages down. Liam sat on a rockin' chair.

"You in yo twenties, but you 'bout old."

He laughed. "Yes, ma'am…"

"But you grillin' so we straight," she said.

Liam stood up an' waved for her to take his seat.

"You stay doin' the most, huh? You ain't need ta jump an' do shi…stuff…for me like dat. I'm jus'…"

"'Course I do, Miss Jewels," he replied, shakin' his head like she's actin' a fool.

"You 'bout stubborn like an' ol' man, too."

He shrugged. "I suppose. But I guess I'm gonna be up an' down at the grill, so you should have somewhere ta sit. Besides, you're my guest. It'd be rude."

"*Oh*, I see. I went from wearin' yo shirts an' sleepin' in yo bed, but now I'm *jus' a guest*, huh?" She bobbed her head an' waved her finger.

Liam choked on his spit. Now it was Jewels' turn to laugh. White boys stay nervous when a black girl gets loud.

"You sweet, Liam. I'm finna sit. Go on, do yo thang. Only time I ever sat in one of these was at Cracker Barrel, but it was after they's closed, so all of 'em was chained an' wouldn't bounce right."

"You ain't never sat in a rockin' chair?"

She shook her head. "Dang, this like a swing. Aight. Tight. Oh, an' this cushion be comfy as hell...oh..." A hand flew up to her mouth. "My bad. Can I say dat now?"

Liam grinned. "Miss Jewels, you're somethin' else, girl."

He flipped the hot dogs.

"You wanna take a walk after supper, down by the river."

"There's a river?"

"Yeah, but don't worry. The gators usually stay on the other side, away from the road."

She laughed at first, but when he didn't, she stopped.

"You fo real? There's gators up in there? Uh-uh! I ain't goin' nowhere near dat!"

"You'll be fine."

"Oh, you superman, huh? You gonna wrestle a gator?"

"I walk by it every day on my way to work."

"An' no gators be chasin' you?"

"No, ma'am."

"Maybe they be likin' dark meat?"

"Dark or white, they don't like the taste of truck tires. They stay away from the roadside of the river, but we can see 'em from the docks, if you want."

"Fo real?" She sounded more excited this time.

He nodded, flippin' the dogs, again.

~*~

After dinner, Jewels talked more about Indy an' the bus ride down to Mississippi while they walked down the side of the road, under the mossy oaks and the magnolias with their white blossoms. Liam hardly got the chance to say a handful of words before they reached the four-way corner by Marco's.

"Hey, tha's that place we's at wit' Tamra," she said.

"Yes ma'am. This here's the big city of Harrison."

She laughed.

"I bet it's nothin' like Indy, is it?"

"No," she replied. "Not even close." *Why'd she sound sad?*

"Missin' home?"

Pssh! "This place is nice. Indy be too wild! Thugs stay trappin' on 10th. You stay walkin', but you don't walk at night."

"That's rough," he replied.

"Tha's life…"

"Well, a girl like you'll get bored here quick, I'd reckon," Liam said.

"A girl like *me?*" When she said it, he heard how it sounded.

"Big city…," he explained. "You're a big city gal. Might look borin' to you."

"Well, I *do* like me some ice cream, Mr. King," she said, puttin' on her best southern accent. *Actually, it wasn't all that bad, either.*

"All the *Mr.* Kings' are my secon' cousins an' whatnot. They own all the nice fields on the other side of Harrison. I'm jus' Liam, ma'am."

"Well, if I'm a ma'am, then you're a Mr. King, feel me?"

"Aight then, *Miss* Jewel. What sorta ice cream you like?"

Strands of light bulbs danced overhead in the breeze as they passed the benches to order at the sliding glass windows. More than a few familiar faces watched as they walked.

Liam waved. Paige an' Katy looked like they'd been in the middle of an argument when they saw him, but if Cora Lynn noticed she didn't seem ta care as far as Liam could tell.

"Hey, Ms. Jewel," she said, slippin' off the bench to rush up to them. "How're ya likin' Harrison so far?"

"Yeah, it's tight. All I done is eat, so…"

"Lots of good food," she agreed. "That's why I'm so fat." She'd changed from her church clothes into a pair of jean shorts rolled up near mid-thigh an' a shirt that read, *Southern Belle Fishin'*.

"Girl, you ain't fat, you thick. Boys like thick girls. Stay thick baby-girl, dem boys'll come when it gets cold."

Cora Lynn giggled, lickin' her cone.

"Not *all* boys," Paige said, suddenly there. "Some like thin girls, huh Liam?"

"Y'all goin' down to Spring Break?" Katy asked, when Liam didn't respond right away.

"No," Jewel and Liam replied at the same time. For some reason they smiled.

"Jus' a walk," Liam added.

"He's gonna keep goin', but I gotta get me some o' dis, so I can have somethin' to throw at a gator if it starts chasin' me. What's a *malt?* Sounds like an ol' man's name. Uncle Malt."

Cora Lynn laughed so hard she snorted.

~*~

"Dem lil' girls finna get you in trouble, Mr. King," Jewels said once they continued on. "They what —fourteen?"

"Sixteen, seventeen? I don't really know," Liam replied. "Nah. They're harmless."

"Yeah, those two stay eyein' me like I stole they man. That Cora Lynn though, she's fried. I bet I could smack her an' she'd stay with a smile. The only thang make her mad is if I'd taken her ice cream."

"Yeah, she's a sweetheart. I've known her family since forever. Played ball with her older brother 'fore he joined the army. They were close with my folks before my folks left to do mission work."

"Ain't a mission where you stay the night? Wit' like beds an' food?" she asked. "We got mission houses in Indy where homeless sleep. They scary though. Lots o' druggies up in 'ere."

Liam didn't want to know how Jewels knew that. He shoved the images from his mind at the sight of her pretty face and braided hair with strands of purple. How much had her gold-brown eyes seen, he didn't wanna know, not really. Deep down, he prayed God might take those memories from her too.

"Missions is how churches send people to different countries to tell people about Jesus. My parents saw a need in Haiti, so they moved to open a school an' orphanage there."

"So, that's why they moved? They doin' God work. That's tight. Why didn't you go, too?"

Liam wanted to tell her. He'd never shared the whole story with anyone before, but there's somethin' 'bout Jewels —her life an' struggles— made him feel like she'd understand more than anyone in Harrison. He heard the tires squealin' like it was yesterday. No one saw the kid crossin' the road.

"You jus' wanted tha' nice house all to yo-self, huh?" She elbowed him with a smile. "Dress girls up in yo shirts an' take 'em ta church?"

Liam smiled, shaking his head.

"I ain't playin' 'bout dem lil' girls though. They trouble. Lil' girls in they feelin's be crazy, like kill some-boy crazy. You big an' strong, but they crazy. Crazy finna win 'at fight!"

"Paige an' Katy are jus' crushin'. I remember bein' their age an' all about an older girl, too. I's crazy 'bout 'er. Did all kinds o' stupid stuff to impress her."

"*Okay!* Lil' Mr. King comin' out tha' shell. Aight. But she wanted them older boys, huh?"

He nodded.

"What happened?"

Liam thought about how to answer for a secon' an' the silence must've been too much for Jewels.

"You ain't gotta…"

"No," he replied. It was hard to say, to hear himself speak to someone about it after all these years. "I…," he shrugged. "He was a good friend an' they were happy. Things happened, so we jus' kinda stopped talkin'."

"Life, huh?" she asked, swipin' a few braids from her face.

"Yeah, I reckon."

"So, yo girl done lef' an' yo folks? Why you stayin'? Why you ain't in the army or somethin' like yo friends?"

"I dunno. I mean, I thought about it. Prayed 'bout it. Almost signed up once, but somebody talked me out of it. I guess I jus' feel like there's still somethin' here for me. Things I need to do. I take college classes, been workin' on my degree. I have another semester an' I'm finished."

Jewels nodded. "Well, I'm glad you stayed," she said. "Ain't no way I's gonna walk by no gators without my Superman."

9

IRONCLAD

MONDAY

Davis lifted the can of screws, askin' where the ol' man wanted it..

"By the porch," he replied.

He sifted through the two folded tarps 'til he found the handsaw, then lifted it up.

"Toss 'em both in Pearly an' grab the sawz-all," the ol' man replied.

Davis nodded.

"You seem quiet today. Got yer mind on somethin'?"

Allie had been off most of the day, away somewhere babysittin' some lil' girl. He saw 'em head out the back door as soon as they pulled in the drive. Ms. Luanne had kept 'em stocked with tea an' snacks, an' even made 'em sammiches with Crawtaters for lunch. More than once, Davis had snuck aroun' the house to see if he could catch a glimpse of her somewhere, but only a long trail wandered away from the shed toward the woods.

"Jus' wonderin' what all we've got planned to do," he half-lied. He did wanna know, but the truth was he'd hoped he could see more of Allie, too. There's somethin' 'bout pretty girls made a fella wanna work jus' a lil' harder.

"Thought we had a deal?" the ol' man replied, misunderstanding.

Davis grinned. "Oh, we do! An' I aim to collect, too." He slapped his stomach.

"Oh yeah, huh? Might wanna get ta work then, 'cause yer work's lookin' more like regular fries than *seasoned* ones."

"Ain't my fault you forgot the wood glue for the porch rails."

"Forgot the..."

"Will you fellas give me a hand up 'ere?" Ms. Luanne called down from the upstairs window. "I need some muscles for a minute."

They started toward the door before the ol' man waved him off. "She said me, not you."

"She said *fellas*," Davis corrected.

"She said *muscles*," he replied. "...not noodles."

They wiped their feet on the mat, an' Davis took his hat off like the ol' man. He wasn't sure why, but seein' his pap do it jus' made him feel awkward not doin' it. They walked through the livin' room, to a set of stairs, then up. It climbed to a landing with pictures on both sides, then turned again for another set. The ol' man pointed to a couple, ones he'd seen somewhere before, but when —Davis didn't know. An old man —Ms. Luanne's husband, likely— stood in a uniform with a tilted hat with two silver bars on it. In another one, he stood beside a plane in a mechanic's jumpsuit.

71

"Mr. Quaves was a pilot in Vietnam," the old man said. "Retired an' settled down here. He was some fella. Tol' great stories."

How'd you know him? What happened to him? Is that how you know Ms. Luanne? Davis didn't get to ask any of his questions. A frail form stood at the top of the stairs with her hands on her hips an' an impatient look on her face.

"Well, you gals gonna take all day fartin' 'round? I could-a moved the durned thang myself by now."

The ol' man chuckled. "Well, you know how hard it is to get these kids movin'...like herdin' cats."

"Stray cats," she mumbled. Davis walked by an' Ms. Luanne pushed him a lil' with a raspy chuckle. "I shoot stray cats."

This part of the house seemed different than the rest, smelled better too.

"Allie'd get all sorts o' flustered she found out y'all's up 'ere, but she ain't home, so...tough titties!"

Houses were different than trailers. Everyone knew that. What most folks didn't know, or didn't thank about, where how different the furniture was between the two. It'd always been somethin' that stuck out to Davis. You could hear your own feet walkin' in a trailer, echoin' through the halls or under, even from the outside, but the hallways were wider in houses, an' in almost everyone he'd ever been in had those long narrow tables with a single lil' drawer or four or five picture frames on it. They didn't do nothin' but jus' hold pictures or flowers, but they looked nice next to long rugs. Trailers might have carpet or linoleum, but didn't usually have rugs, an' never had a narrow table unless it was in the dinin' room. He always found himself starin' at 'em for some reason. Seemed like a waste o' money to him, but he couldn't deny they were sorta pretty, too.

Allie at all ages decorated everything. Pigtails an' smiles; piggyback on her ol' man. Dresses an' recitals. Beaches an' sandcastles. The old man didn't seem as interested eyein' the pictures here as they passed a couple closed doors, probably closets, maybe a bedroom or two, before Ms. Luanne pointed an ol' crooked finger toward a half-moved bookshelf at the end of the hall, stickin' out halfway from an open door. It was large an' the angle had made it almost impossible to fit into the hall from the room without scrapin' somethin'.

"D'ya build it in the room?" the ol' man asked as Davis thought the same thing.

"Nope," Ms. Luanne replied, matter-of-factly. "Carried it up 'ere with Catfish all by myself, but tha' was way back when you's likely his age, Robbie."

"Well, noodles 'ere ain't half as tough as you were, an' he's barely stronger than he smells, but we'll get 'er done," the ol' man replied. Davis just shook his head.

"I want it in Catfish's ol' sittin' room. You 'member which one that was, don't ya?"

"Yes'am," he replied.

"You'll see where I want it. Cain't miss it."

"You leavin'?" he asked.

"Jus' swingin' down by the river an' the grocery store. Gotta get me a pig's butt for a roast an' some taters. I swear that girl can cook jus' fine, but I still gotta make the yummy stuff from time to time, or I'm up a creek without a paddle."

"Well, we'll get this done an' get outta yer hair. Told this turd I'd get him Marco's."

"Aight. No rush. Jus' head out the back when yer done."

"Yes'am, he replied.

73

She tossed her hand up in a wave an' winked at Davis as she walked by, then slapped him on the arm for no good reason. "There," she said. "Let that'n grow on ya."

The ol' man shook his head chucklin'.

"What?"

"The look on yer face."

"She's somethin' else," Davis whispered, half wonderin' if the old woman could still hear him, an' what might happen if she did.

"These were good people," he mumbled. His eyes looked distant again, saddened by somethin' as his rough hands started to grab the shelf. They stopped when they touched it an' slowly rubbed it, like he's rememberin' something.

"Were?" Davis echoed. It took a breath or two before the ol' man shook the thoughts away an' nodded.

"Yeah, bad things happen to good folks, bud. An' sometimes good people do bad things on accident to good folks thinkin' they're doin' good things, too."

Davis got lost in the words before he un-jumbled 'em in his ears, but by then he'd already wiggled past the monster shelf an' into the room where he could get a good hold of it. When the words finally made sense, the moment had passed, an' the thought of bringing it up again didn't seem right. When it was finally in the hall, he walked away to one of the closed doors, opened it, and peeked inside. Davis waited for the ol' man to come back before a sharp nod told him to lift, again. They wiggled it in like cuttin' a pie, then set it down gingerly without scuffin' the old wood floor.

"Readin' room, huh? I thought only rich folks had these?" Davis said.

"Ol' Catfish was a pretty smart fella. Big history buff. Did a lot o' studyin' an' even taught U.S. History over at the college for....*shew*...years, I think. Hey, look here," he said. The excitement in his voice startled Davis. It wasn't often the ol' man got excitable. Flustered, sure, but rarely excitable. A fingertip pointed to a spread of framed pictures on one o' those narrow tables along the wall beneath a bunch of other old ones. On it set a replica of an old ship tha' looked like a submarine or somethin'.

Catfish looked older, heavier too, but still had the same crooked grin. Beside him stood a young man who looked about Allie's age, mid-twenties. They were posing in front of a ship that matched the replica on the table.

"That's me an' him," he said with a laugh. "I didn't even know he had this."

"You knew 'em pretty good, huh?" Davis said, surprised, bending over to see through the dustiness of it. "Him an' Ms. Luanne?"

"Yeah, we spent a good year together, the two of us. Your grandpa knew him when he was a youngster, an' when he passed, ol' Catfish an' I got close for a lil' while before I started workin' more at the shop. That summer, he took me on a drive up to Vicksburg. That's where this picture's from. It's called an Ironclad ship. They used 'em in the Civil War."

"I ain't never seen anything like this," Davis said. "When did he pass?"

"'Bout two years after they got Allie-girl."

"...got?"

"They never had any kids o' their own. They got Allie-girl when she was young, adopted her from a niece, I think."

"Ms. Luanne said she knew momma," Davis said, suddenly. "Said she's the bes' thang ever came from up north."

"Well," he chuckled. "Ms. Luanne's a lotta thangs, but a liar ain't one of 'em. I reckon you'd have to care what others think, an' she don't!"

When the ol' man didn't take the conversation any further, an' started for the door, Davis did. "Allie said she knew me when I's younger, too, but I don't remember her."

"Oh, well," he started, but Davis could tell somethin' seemed forced, almost like he was chokin' on what to say.

"They knew you an' your momma good, buddy. I, uh, I wasn't aroun' a lot then. Worked quite a bit durin' those years, drove a lot makin' service calls for the shop when business got slow. Stayed busy." His words trailed off as that distant look washed over his face again, like a long drawl of buttermilk. "...*too* busy," he mumbled.

A memory flashed in Davis' mind then, one he'd never had, almost like a dream. It was a gray and white truck with large tool-boxes on the side, parked in the old part of the driveway near the magnolias by the horseshoe pit. He remembered the shiny white rocks glistenin' in the drive where only crabgrass and cattails grew now. There was a blue truck there too, like his, only with a roll bar an' spotlights on top.

"Did you have Pearly back then?" Davis asked as they walked outta the room and back toward the stairs.

"Nope. Didn't get ol' Pearly 'til you were, oh, ten or so, I think."

"Did you have a blue truck back then?"

He stopped a few steps down an' turned with a look in his eye Davis had never seen, a mixture of sad or afraid, somethin' he couldn't place. "Blue truck? Why d'you..."

"When you's talkin' 'bout drivin' for the shop I had a memory, I think. I saw a gray an' white dually with toolboxes...an' a blue pickup in the drive."

Hmm, he replied with a strangled grin. "Well, that memory of yours is pretty sharp, bud. You nailed my service truck. Doesn't a day go by I'd ever feel desperate enough to say I miss that ol' hunk o' junk! Speakin' o' service...we bes' beat the rush at Marco's if you want yer paycheck before eight."

"Sounds good ta me," Davis said, though a few more questions still lingered.

Picture frames passed as they made their way to Pearly; a pony-tail hangin' out the back of a softball cap; frogs in front of muddy faces; a high school Allie fieldin' a ground ball, then a gorgeous homecoming dress with a boy in a suit went by in a blur. Another few lingered there, too, ones Davis hadn't seen, distracted by the Allie in the homecoming dress.

Allie an' a boy covered in mud, huggin' in front of a muddy blue truck by the river.

10

NO AN' MAYBE.

MONDAY

Liam stretched his legs in the back yard, beneath the magnolias by the porch when Jewels took her seat on the rockin' chair. Coffee cup in hand, somethin' tol' Liam she hadn't missed readin' the notes he'd left for her.

"You up early," she said.

"I take a run every now an' 'en through town, by the post office, then back. Then, I hop in the shower an' head off ta work."

"Oh, yeah," she said, suddenly realizing. "I didn't think 'bout that. I mean, I knew you pro'lly did, but where you work at? The church?"

"Naw, I work at the Fun Park, down by the beach on the weekends durin' the summer, an' over the breaks. It's how I stay busy when I'm not at college. Mr. Montgomery an' his brother own it."

"Okay, okay. Monte a ladies' man *an'* he's loaded. Dang. Ol' man's got it. I'm 'bout ta leave my shirt daddy for a suga daddy."

Liam grinned, shaking his head. He wiped his face with a hand towel on the picnic table, then took a deep breath. "Hear that? All the crickets an' cicadas?"

"The bugs?"

"Yeah," he replied with a laugh. "When you hear 'em all loud an' hollerin' this early in the mornin', it usually means we're in for a hot one."

"Don't worry, I ain't goin' on no nature walk with gators an' snakes all out. I'm waitin' on Superman to come home, first."

"You could come, you know? With me. To work. If you want. I could get you in on some rides for free an' the boardwalk isn't far. If you walk a few miles or so, there's even a mall in the next city over."

He could tell she struggled to say no, but it was all the same to him. Some time apart might be good, help 'er clear up her thoughts a bit.

"Thanks though," she said, liftin' her cup. "An' them spicy sausages was fire!"

"There's plenty of food layin' 'roun' for sammiches an' whatnot for lunch, too. I usually pick somethin' up with Mr. Montgomery on Mondays. If you need anything, his number is by the phone in the livin' room."

"I'll be aight," she replied. "You jus' do your thang, Mr. King."

~*~

"So you jus' left her at the house?"

Mr. Montgomery didn't sound like he didn't approve, more like he hadn't heard what Liam said over the thumpin' of the music blastin' from every car an' truck jammed bumper to bumper up an' down the beach. Spring Break brought all sorts of crazy to these parts, an' though the old man didn't mind the boom of the business, like most old country folk he wasn't fond of the extra noise.

"I tol' her she could come. Figured you wouldn't mind chattin' with her an' lettin' her on the rides. I even thought she'd like walkin' up an' down the beach."

"An' she said no, huh?"

Liam shrugged.

"Likely wanted some space is all," Mr. Montgomery said with a nod. He took his seat beneath the umbrella at the circular concrete benches an' lifted his puny ice cream cup, shakin' his head.

"These thangs still taste good, but I'll be darned if they don't get smaller an' smaller while the prices get higher an' higher. Almos' a truck payment for a decent meal 'round 'ere."

"Missin' Harrison?" Liam joked.

"Can't beat Marco's, that's fer sure."

"Travis at school?"

"Naw, he's with some friends today. Headin' down to do some fishin' at the river."

"Pine side or,"

"Oak side," Mr. Montgomery shook his head an' stopped as a brain freeze set in.

"Don't worry, it'll pass quick," Liam teased.

"I can see tha' gal's been brushin' up on yer wit. You gotta stay sharp 'roun' that'n. She's a spitfire."

Liam got quiet, thinkin', but Mr. Montgomery didn't miss the opportunity.

"What's yer plan, son? She ought not stay with ya for too long a spell. Folks get throwin' their noses in other folks' businesses too quick 'round Harrison. You know that better than most."

"I sent my folks a message, an' left a message with Mrs. Gina for Pastor Sam to gimme a call." He shrugged. "To be honest, I ain't sure. She don't seem to wanna go back to Indy, an' I don't know what ta do for her other than keep her safe an' give her somewhere to be."

"You like her?"

Liam wasn't ready for that. He stammered.

No. Maybe. Both answers came at once. Gold brown eyes shone like a shiny piece of toffee with a flash of purple braids in front of mocha skin. She was beautiful, to be sure. But she wasn't...*his*. She had a beauty, but not the same one Liam had always sought —the one he thought about from time to time when the clouds rolled in from the gulf with a cool wind an' he's inclined to curlin' up on the porch swing with his arms wrapped 'round someone, an' the sound of the rain fallin' on the porch came to mind. The same beauty that'd captured his heart for years, always lingerin' jus' a lil' too far away. He'd only shared a handful of memories like those with her, ones he relived over an' over again like they were yesterday. When he finally shook his head, Mr. Montgomery didn't tease him as he'd expected. There'd been another question in there somewhere, tossin' 'round in tha' head of his, an' whatever it'd been, had been answered by Liam's silence.

"You jus' keep doin' right by her, son," he finally said, scrapin' every last morsel of the chocolate from the bottom of his tiny cup, shakin' his head in disapproval once again at how itty-bitty it'd been. "We know, an' Jesus knows," he added, tossin' him a wink. "E'rybody else can take their gossip an' shove it where the sun don't shine for all I care."

"Liam," he called a few hours later from the door with a wave. He snatched up the rag beside the go-kart an' wiped his greasy hands on it as he walked.

"Yessir?"

"I'm headed into Harrison to get Travis. You want me ta swing by an' see if Jewel's changed her mind? She might wanna come down to the beach for the evenin' an' ride some rides."

"Sure."

"Well, you an' the temps hold down the fort, an' I'll be back in a jiffy."

Mr. Montgomery always called the seasonal workers 'temps', an' most of the time didn't even bother to learn their names. "Got too much I already forget. Ain't got any room up here for nonsense like kids' names. They're jus' gonna quit in a week or so anyhow," he'd say.

Felt like no time at all had passed when Mr. Montgomery came back with Travis an' Jewel. By the smile on both of their faces, an' the rosy cheeks on Travis, it didn't take Liam too long to get to the bottom of things.

"Messin' with my buddy?" he asked Jewel.

She acted like Liam had smacked her. "Naw, I's jus' sayin' if Fancy Nancy don' snatch him up, I'm finna finesse her man."

"Liam, tell 'em shut up 'er somethin'. They're-they're annoyin' me," Travis stammered.

"Y'all leave my buddy alone or I'm gonna get y'all on the Ferris Wheel an' trap you at the top!"

Travis' mouth fell open. He looked to 'em wide-eyed with a smile. "Do it, Liam!"

"I might, if they don't quit pesterin'."

Jewel craned her head up at it, an' part of Liam wondered if the thought hadn't scared her a lil'.

"Don't like these?"

"It's...uh...high."

He laughed. "Yeah, that's sorta the point, I think."

She smacked him on the arm.

"Hey, I'm gonna be in that area most of the night, runnin' the fast track of go-karts. It's away from everything else. See those big rolls of tickets in those kids' hands? Find a group an' jus' follow 'em 'round. I'll tell all the fellas you're with me an' they'll let you on whatever ya want all night."

"For free?"

He nodded.

"An' Monte don' care?"

"Nah! If he does, that'd be a first. I came in early today to change some tires on the karts, so he'll be lettin' me go aroun' six. We can get dinner at Marco's or Fancy's, if you want?"

Jewels shrugged, scannin' the place over. The lights weren't on yet, but he could see the inner kid buzzin' with the sounds of the rides an' the crowds of folks laughin' on the goofy golf course. Someone's ball had bounced off of somethin' an' was rollin' half way across the parkin' lot. The thought hadn't occurred to Liam that she'd never been to anything like the Fun Park before. He'd assumed a bigger city like Indy had everything better than their lil' old town. After all, when Mr. Montgomery an' his brother bought it from a travelin' carnival nobody expected it to become somethin' permanent on the beachfront. A dozen years later, an' it still went strong.

"Oh," she said before he started away, "one of your girlfriends said hey."

He laughed. "My girlfriends? Which one?"

"I dunno. I didn't take no message or nothin'. She was talkin' to Monte when we's pickin' up Travis, an' when she heard I's stayin' wit you, she said to say hi. Said somethin' 'bout how you two knew each other."

Hmm. "Did you see her at church the other day?"

Jewels looked at him like '*didn't I say I don't know*' an' shook her head. "Naw, but she's got it goin' on. Girl was fine. You need ta get her in church an' put a ring on 'at."

"Now you sound like Tamra almos' every time we do anything together," he said, laughin'.

"Yeah, all us black girls soun' the same," she replied, cockin' her head with her attitude.

Spitfire, he heard Mr. Montgomery say in his mind, again. *Don't light a fuse.*

From a distance, Liam spotted Jewel spinnin' on the tilt-o-whirl with Travis, then again on the tiniest roller coaster known to man. The circle wasn't any bigger than a single-wide trailer, but the longer the conductor left the lever wide open, the more momentum it gained. As the afternoon turned to evenin', the ride times would get a lil' shorter an' shorter to keep the lines movin', Liam knew, but the smile on Jewel's face infectiously spread to his.

You like her? He heard Mr. Montgomery ask again in his mind. An' truth be tol' Liam wasn't so sure. It wasn't long after the timer tripped an' the neon lights shot on like an' explosion an' that bright wide smile exploded with 'em.

"It'll be gettin' dark soon. Y'ought ta head on back, unless y'all wanna ride?" Mr. Montgomery offered once another temp relieved him at the fast track.

"I'll ask, but I think she'll like the walk after bein' cooped up all mornin'."

Jewel got off the bumper cars, grabbin' her neck.

"Folks be gettin' crazy on 'em bumpin' cars. They takin' they road rage out or somethin'. Tha' ol' lady up in 'ere tryin' to throw some kids from they car. I ain't tryna get insurance. Dang!"

"Sounds like you need a good slushy from the counter an' a surprise ride."

Huh. "Do I look like a girl you wanna surprise wit' somethin'?"

Liam grinned. "Maybe. I did see how much you liked the roller coaster."

Jewels smiled. "Yeah, I ain't never been on one 'em. They tight. The county fair in Indy be tryin' to get yo whole tax return for a ticket. So, I ain't never been. Doin' all this for free…"

"Well, let's get a slushy then I'm gonna ask you to do somethin' crazy."

"Crazy?"

"Crazy."

"Like cray-cray crazy, or wild an' Mr. King crazy? 'Cause not puttin' suga in yo tea or salt on yo burger be 'bout as crazy as you white boys get 'roun' hur." She waved her finger for emphasis and bobbed her head with an expression that made him laugh. Even she couldn't keep a straight face.

Uhhh… "The secon' one," he said, hopin' she'd agree.

"Aight then," she said. "What flavas y'all got?"

Liam gasped an' pointed at her. "You said yer first southern word!"

"Y'all?" she repeated it.

He nodded. "See. Makin' you a southerner. Pretty soon you're gonna be sayin' *reckon* an' *hollerin'*, an' all sorts o' whatnot."

"Okay, you actin' a fool now. Take *y'all* for right now. We gots to negotiate on dem other ones."

He walked behind her an' covered her eyes all the way past the tilt-o-whirl, then spun her twice, an' kept walkin' toward the sand, where the Fun Park met the beach. Travis walked beside him, gigglin', his hand cupped over his mouth to keep from blurtin' too much, an' to show Liam he understood what he meant when he'd held up one finger to be quieter.

Liam winked at the newbie an' nodded for him to open the door slowly.

"Okay," he said. "There's two steps, then a small platform. "The tilt-o-, I mean, it's a lil' wobbly, but the seats are cushioned, so it should be aight. Don't worry, I got ya."

Jewels smirked at his near mishap, but all the surety in her drained away when the newbie pulled the lever an' Liam let his hands go. By the time she started to climb him and complain, it was too late. The Ferris Wheel had started.

Uh-uh! "Liam King! Liam! Oh, dang! Oh, this high! Oh, I don't wanna do this! Noooo!" *Uh-uh!*

Travis jumped up an' down on the sand below clappin' his hands chuckling. Mr. Montgomery stood wipin' the tears from his eyes. The sunset over the beach, ripplin' on the gulf high above the noise of the speakers bumpin' up an' down the highway nearby seemed far away. They went around a few turns before Liam gave him the signal an' it slowed to a stop near the top. Then, they just sat for a few moments, starin' at the water.

"Oooooh, Liam. Oh, Liam. What'd you do? Ohhhh, this is sooo high. I hate you! Make 'm get down! This gonna get stuck! I'm finna roll out into the ocean."

Liam laughed. "Hey. Hey? It's okay. Look. Look out there. Jewel, open your eyes. Look. See that?"

It took a few seconds to convince her, but when she did he pointed to help.

"See the islands out there. There's even an ol' Civil War fort out there, too. I forgot the name of it, but its out there. I've been on this a hundred times, an' operated for thousan's, an' I ain't ne'er…"

He pretended to freak out an' rocked the seat a lil'. Jewel might have beat him to death if she hadn't stopped an' started laughin' at the sight of Travis' laughter echoin' up.

"Do it, again, Liam!" he hollered.

"Oh, you wrong for dat! You 'bout ta get it now!" she threatened with a wagglin' finger after he helped her off the seat gingerly and down the stairs.

"Would you like a…"

"No! An' *you* don't talk to me neither!" she said, pointin' her finger at Mr. Montgomery. "You's hatin' too! I saw you. Y'all suppose ta be protectin' me an' y'all be all tryna kill me up there?"

Mr. Montgomery had to sit down beside the bumper cars to wipe the tears from his eyes. Liam couldn't remember a time he'd seen the old man laugh so hard.

11

GIRLFRIEND-EMIES

MONDAY EVENIN'

Pearly nudged the curb an' rocked back before the ol' man tossed her in park. The phone buzzed in the seat beside him, so Davis glanced at it. *Dillon.* He thought to snatch it up to give'm a good chewin', but figured the conversation could get odd in front of the ol' man, an' quick, if he started askin' the wrong questions. Tha's the thang 'bout livin' in a small town though. Even though secrets could have secrets, somebody somewhere knew more than they should an' talked even more 'bout it than they ought.

As if his own thoughts created 'em, the tongue-twins eyed him from afar. Some fellas joked about how inseparable they were, like a two-headed snake, but Davis knew different. He kept them separated jus' fine.

"Evenin' Mr. Allen," they said as Davis an' the ol' man walked by. They both eyed Davis promising him they'd heard all about his juicy gossip, an' wanted nothin' more than to talk his ears off to get the details. Funny how his phone hadn't blown up with folks worried 'bout him, but word of Dillon's party an' his truck layin' in a ditch had made it everywhere.

He stood at the slidin' window an' made sure the ol' man said 'seasoned', knowin' he'd likely say 'regular' jus' to yank his chain while he chomped on seasoned ones.

"Barq's, first. Shakes later?" he asked.

"You bet," Davis replied.

"I's yankin' yer chain earlier. You did some good hard work today."

Davis didn't know what to say. It wasn't that he didn't appreciate it or nothin', or that he didn't know how ta take a compliment. Every ol' timer gave him a good pat on the back after watchin' one o' his games, but there's somethin' about how the ol' man did it, jus' wasn't the same. He could count on one hand how many times he'd heard him say it in jus' as many years, an' it always had to do with work, never sports, though many of the ol' timers talked 'bout how it ran in his blood, or how the apple didn't fall far from the tree, whatever that meant. As far as Davis knew, he'd never seen or heard his ol' man talk sports outside o' hollerin' at the TV. Even when he's surrounded by all his buddies at the house knockin' back a few beers. In those moments, when the liquid courage brought up the braggin' an' the stories from the good-ol'-days, his ol' man stayed tight lipped while Cheesy an' Buckwheat, his two work buddies, lied about everything under the moon.

"You tryin' to get outta owin' me four more days' worth of Marco's or somethin'?"

The ol' man smirked. "Nah, you'll get all sissified by wins-dee anyhow. Start witherin' in the sun like a weed whinin' 'bout everything. Figured I ought to lie a lil' to keep you motivated, you know,"

"Yeah, I figured," Davis mumbled, shakin' his head.

One of the girls found the opportunity when Cheesy an' Buckwheat rolled up an' hollered at the ol' man to talk shop for a few. She walked past him, then circled back after she pretended to talk to another couple a few tables over.

"Heard about yer truck," Kat said, pouting slightly. Her fingers traced a chain tucked away in the middle of her shirt, a chain that tucked away down low between her cleavage. When Davis noticed, her eyes flashed a 'gotcha' sorta shine.

"How long 'til it's runnin' again?" she asked.

"Why, you miss it or somethin'?"

She grinned.

"It's jus' a lil' banged up is all," he said. "Maybe a week."

"What about the party? Does anybody," she started, but Davis shook his head.

"Nope," he replied, though he was pretty sure his ol' man had a hunch only hadn't said anything about it, yet. The town was too small an' more than one of the men at his shop had kids at the school, too. It was only a matter of time.

"Man, you're lucky," she said. "Your dad's so laid back. If that'd been me, I'd be dead."

"It wasn't *that* bad,"

"I mean my parents," she corrected, shakin' her head. "They'd 've killed me."

"What would they do if they knew about us?"

There was a time when she might've blushed, but now she only smiled.

"I'm jus' glad you weren't in it," Davis said. He meant because of how dead they'd both have been when their parents found out, or if they'd seen what she was wearin' that night. Davis hadn't meant for it to sound sweet an' considerate. When he saw her response, an' the twinkle in her eye, he gave the reel a good yank to make sure the hook set in 'ere.

"So...nobody knows?" he said with a nod to the other girls. "Not even 'em?"

She slipped off the table in front of him slowly an' watched his eyes dart from hers to her legs an' then back.

"Only us," she replied.

~*~

Davis' dad bought two shakes an' they didn't even bother stayin' to drink 'em. It wasn't often they went out in public together. Most of the time Davis drove up an' spent the evenin' with 'em or they'd head down to the river, but with his truck wrecked Cora Lynn hoped everything might change.

No one had *talked* about it, but everybody had seen an' heard about the Green Goblin busted up in a ditch. And that Dillon's party had been the wildest thing the 'River Lair' had ever experienced. With all the police in the town helpin' out with the Spring Breakers, there'd been nothin' to keep 'em from bein' caught. It'd been planned by a genius: Davis Allen.

"What were you two talkin' 'bout all smiley?" Paige asked when Katy came back.

Cora Lynn saw Katy's eyes dart to her like lasers, an' knew why. Katy had tol' her 'bout Davis an' made her promise not to. They were two of the most popular girls in Harrison, an' Cora Lynn wondered if the only reason they had anything to do with her at all wasn't because they all went to church together. It was their thing. Their place. A world away from the rest of the world. To them, it seemed like jus' another place to hang out, but to Cora Lynn it was like a bridge between two worlds, an' she'd finally been invited.

But now that she had, she wasn't so sure she wanted to be.

She hadn't expected all the secrets an' the lies —how quickly she'd learn what the sparkle in Paige's eyes meant as she watched Katy walk away to order a shake. It was a hint of jealousy Katy overlooked. Cora Lynn knew *that* secret too. The secrets they'd both kept about Davis. Paige had been first, but once Katy heard, she wanted what Paige had. 'Course, they were both in secret, an' usually when one or the other had stayed the night with her, but neither girl told Cora Lynn their plan beforehand. They'd both asked to stay the night at her place an' then sneaked out since her house was only a short walk from the river lair. Now that she thought about it, it'd likely been Davis' idea, not theirs. How gross!

Cora Lynn didn't realize it 'til it was too late, but by then she felt used an' stupid and what could she do, tell someone at school? Nobody would believe the ugly, chubby geek over the star softball players. They'd see her ruined overnight at school an' at church.

The more Cora Lynn thought about it, the more she wondered if Davis might've asked her to do the same if she was half as pretty as they were. At first, she'd even had a dream or two about it, but after seein' how he was she didn't care anymore, not really. They weren't her friends, an' he wasn't the type of boy she *really* wanted.

And then, as if her mind made him appear, Liam King walked around the corner.

12

FITTIN' IN

MONDAY EVENIN'

Cora Lynn's gaze lifted from the table to Liam as her frown slid to a smile. It hadn't been the first time he'd seen something hidden there, a rain cloud in a wide-open sky of sunshine and white puffy clouds.

"Evenin' Miss Cora," he said, musterin' a smile. "Everything okay?"

"Hey, Liam," she said sweetly, an' he couldn't help but miss the scratchiness in her throat, like she'd been on the verge of tears or had a dry throat. As always she didn't speak too much —at least, not right away— but nodded up and down emphatically.

"Hey, Miss Jewel," she said.

"Wassup, girl," Jewel replied, though her eyes were already on the overhead menu.

Paige and Katy appeared from the picnic tables, suddenly at the table, but didn't say much. Fat bulbs dangled loosely from wires, drooping between the growing shadows over each table as the sun set behind the towering pines.

Seein' as how they were some of the few people Jewels knew, Liam figured it was more likely than not she'd keep on with her earlier comments 'bout them girls *'stayin' trouble'* for him. At first, he hadn't considered it too much, but now – with the look on Cora Lynn's face an' a quick glance to Katy an' Paige eyein' one another with sudden skeptical glances, he wondered if Jewels hadn't been onto something. But what had Cora Lynn so flustered? Perhaps tha' woman's intuition was a *real* thang, or worse, everyone's worryin' was startin' ta wear on him. With another glance to the masks of Paige and Katy quickly melding back into their usual places, Liam couldn't help but wonder if they hadn't been cuttin' sweet lil' Cora Lynn outta somethin'.

~*~

"Yeah, theys up to somethin'," Jewels said without a doubt. "Even Smiley was actin' all...," she waved her hand around an' Liam understood. He'd seen it on Cora Lynn's face too.

"An' you think it has to do with me?"

"You guilty or somethin', Mr. King?" Jewels replied with an eyebrow over her ice cream cone.

"No," he replied, stirring his chocolate shake.

Mmm-hmm. "You ain't gotta tell me all yo' secrets. I see these lil' white girls all dreamy-eyed. Tryna be Mr. King's queen."

He shook his head.

"Is tha' some red in 'em cheeks, Mr. King? Tryna pretend you ain't all playa. I see you. You ain't 'bouts ta get a side piece playin' all innocent."

"I got more shirts," he replied, crackin' a smile. Jewels almost dropped her cone in shock at his comeback. All he could do was laugh when she shoved him.

94

"*Oh-kay!* You need ta let tha' babysitter wear one. I'm for real!"

"I still don't know who you're talkin' 'bout."

"I forgot. Harrison be so big you done forgot all the girls be all 'bout you, huh?"

Liam shook his head, speechless. There was no right way to win an argument with Jewel.

"Oh, you ain't even tryna hide tha' red now. If yo' ol' man country-self had a phone I'd baby mama through yo contacts an' show you." Jewels gasped. "That's it! *That's* why you ain't got one. You be's hidin' 'em from one another like a pimp. Mr. King really is a playa, y'all! Ain't no trace o' yo' game, huh? You good!"

Liam could only shake his head an' laugh while Jewels kept going back an' forth with herself, makin' him more an' more embarrassed as she did.

"Okay, okay," he said, hushin' her. "What would you think 'bout comin' to work with me tomorrow. I'll check, but I'm sure Mr. Montgomery would give ya a ride to the mall or somethin' to get you outta this place for a day. I mean, I bet you're goin' nuts surrounded by woods."

Jewels finished laughing and shrugged at the offer.

"I ain't told you thank you as much as I should've," she said suddenly. "You're...you really is a good man, Liam. I ain't never met one like you. You make me feel like I'm in a movie where some black girl meets one o' them foreign guys an' er'body cries at the end. My girl Shayla back in Indy stay watchin' dem lame as-, *uh*...kind-a movies."

After bein' teased an' tormented merely breaths before, Liam wasn't sure how to respond genuinely. All he thought to do was rock into her, his large frame pushin' her unexpectedly like a brother and a sister resolvin' an argument.

"You're worth it," he said.

When she started to shake her head, he leaned into her, again.

"Really, I mean it," he added, but this time he tossed an arm over her shoulder. "I knew you were worth it from the moment I first saw ya, an' how they'd treated ya. At first, I thought no one deserved to be treated like that, but now that I know you better, I know no one should've ever treated *you* like that, either. An' no matter what, you 'ave ta promise me you'll never let anyone try ta get away with treatin' you like anything other than a daughter of God, again. You deserve a good Godly man, Jewels. Never settle for anyone less!"

Cora Lynn didn't feel right ignorin' Paige an' Katy when they bombarded her with question after question 'bout what Liam had to say. But she'd finally started seein' more an' more what everyone said 'bout them to be true. All her old friends at school an' church had told her they were jus' gonna use her ta get what they wanted, an' now Cora Lynn knew they'd been right. Now, she'd be forced to either continue in the shame of bein' used knowin' good an' well they were doin' what she didn't really want ta do —even though there were plenty of boys at the river who'd settle for even her, which she wasn't *really* interested in, truth be tol'– or doin' the next hardest thing, goin' back to bein' a nobody all over again. After the first guy stopped makin' out with her one night so he could stumble away to puke somewhere and pass out drunk, she realized the whole popularity of high school to be more of a joke than all the glitter she'd seen from the outside lookin' in.

But if she turned her back on Paige and Katy, she'd likely be a nobody who'd burned not one but two bridges, an' both of 'em at her only two places she had, school an' church. In one world, she'd been a nobody tryin' ta fit-in. Paige an' Katy had given her that with lil' makeovers and waitin' for her between classes. But at church, durin' the bible studies an' the pledges an' Lady nights, she'd been the one helpin' them. To her, fittin' in at school had always been somethin' she'd dreamed of, but now –now that she saw it for what it all meant an' what it all led to– Cora Lynn wondered if she'd been seein' things backwards. Maybe they'd been the ones who'd needed her help all this time. And now, as the final scent of Liam lifted away from her shoulders where he'd hugged her before he left, an' she watched him walk away down the street beside Jewel, Cora Lynn thought maybe it was time she helped them a lil' bit more; only in a way they needed, but likely didn't truly want.

But before she did – before she made *too* many decisions – she'd need to ask the only girl she knew she could trust if her ideas were right. An' while Cora Lynn knew she didn't know Paige or Katy, an' she likely wouldn't know all the details –which was fine by her– she at least cared about Cora Lynn, an' had always given her good advice whenever she asked Cora Lynn to babysit or they saw one another at the river an' met to walk around from time to time.

Lost in her thoughts, Cora Lynn didn't listen too much to the juicy gossip of Paige an' Katy, an' thought instead about her plan as they waited 'til their moms came and picked 'em up from Marco's. Once she was alone, a few messages was all it took before Allie finally replied and agreed to meet with her. Now, Cora Lynn thought, it was time ta see everything made right.

13

THE RIVER LAIR

MONDAY EVENIN'

"Cheesy an' Buckwheat wanna come by an' talk shop for a lil' bit," the ol' man said on the ride home.

"Aight," Davis replied, not really sure why the ol' man had decided to tell him. Those two jus' sorta showed up whenever they had a mind to anyhow. To him, they were like uncles he didn't have to like, an' he saw 'em jus' about as often as folks who had uncles. Davis did have one, a brother of his mom's, but he lived all the way out in Colorado. That's all Davis knew about him, except for a rare phone call 'ere an' there, but even one of those had been years ago before he had kids of his own.

"Is it aight if I slip out an' take a drive?" Davis asked.

There was a lil' hesitation before the ol' man nodded an' tossed him the keys ta Pearly. "Where ya headed?" he asked.

"Dillon messaged me. Said somethin' 'bout them doin' some work on the field before practices next week. Thought

I might slip by an' see," he shrugged. "Jus' cruise a lil'. Dillon might meet me an' we might toss the ball a lil' before practices start next week."

"Aight. Nothin' stupid. Bring her back, ya hear? Flip mine an' we'll be up a creek."

Davis hadn't lied about any of it. The school *was* workin' on the dugouts an' the diamond; and he *had* planned on tossin' the ball with Dillon more before practices started, but he'd had somethin' else on his mind, too.

Davis eased Pearly into the small abandoned parkin' lot beneath the mossy oaks near the River Lair jus' as Katy jogged from where she was hidin' to the truck an' hopped in. Before they could even kiss, flashlights danced down a wooded path. Somebody, whoever it was, was runnin' through the woods. Windows cracked, they could hear the gigglin', an' at first, they thought it was gonna be another couple tryin' ta find a good make out spot, but all that flew out the window when Allie burst out. Davis sat up, confused. *How'd she know where the River Lair was*, he wondered? Hadn't he an' Dillon found it when they's huntin' las' November? To his knowledge, nobody even knew it existed 'til they'd started havin' parties out there.

The look on his face must've stirred Katy 'cause she perked up, too.

"What? Who is that? You know her?"

Before he could reply, Cora Lynn slipped out from the path behind her, laughin' an' shakin' her head as winded as Allie. They both laughed.

"If that'd been somethin' scary," Cora Lynn said, "you would-a jus' let me die!"

"Uh, it *was* somethin' scary!" Allie replied. "Raccoons are scary. Bye! I got a flashlight an' a path. You'll be missed, missy."

"That's what you'd tell my folks?"

"Yep. I'd add a lil' somethin' 'bout you how said, *'Go! Save yerself.'* Or how you bravely fought off three of 'em while I escaped an' saved the two lil' kids on the way or somethin', jus' so they'd be really, extra proud of ya, an' all. I wouldn't let ya die screamin' or anything in my stories."

They laughed an', as Davis and Katy watched, turned an' slowly walked away toward the beach area where the pale moonlight shown down on the slow-movin' water, tricklin' around the river rocks. Hopefully, they'd head back into the woods down-a-ways an' circle back to where they came from. He wasn't sure what'd happen if she saw Pearly. Would she say somethin' to her momma? Would either of 'em say anything to his ol' man? Before the wreck he hadn't been too worried, but for some reason Davis felt like things were changin'.

Why, of all the girls, an' all the times, would —of all people— Cora Lynn show Allie the River Lair now, he wondered? He almost shook his head at the nonsense of it all, but couldn't bring himself to —a sundress under hazel eyes was callin' his name. He'd 'ave to make sense out of it all some other time.

When Davis got home, Cheesy and Buckwheat were gone an' the ol' man was rootin' around in the shed, probably sortin' through tools or organizin' his stuff nobody ever seemed to return. Occasionally, they'd trade him somethin' they lost or broke with somethin' he didn't really need, then he'd have to sell that and save up the money to buy back whatever they'd lost or broken. Over the past couple years alone, he'd lost count of how many nice tools —a table saw, an arch welder, an' even a power torque wrench— had 'disappeared' with some stupid story that left the ol' man without another tool for a season. *Jus' 'ave ta start lockin' up my stuff 'round the shop, I suppose*, the ol' man would complain, shakin' his head.

Instead of makin' up any more lies to cover where he'd been, or with who, Davis decided to slip inside and take a shower. They'd be up early an' back out in the mornin' anyhow, an' seein' as how the ol' man wouldn't be takin' a shower anytime soon, he figured he'd beat him to it.

The light from the fan above the oven cast a faint outline of the cedar chest on the bedroom floor again. He went from dang near forgettin' about the thang altogether to seein' it out from underneath the bed twice in one week, an' with the ol' man up to his ears in the shed Davis eased in the room like a burglar without turnin' on the light. To his surprise it was still open. Even when he had seen it out before, which was nearly never, the ol' man seldom left it open. Two boxes of old perfume stood out all pink an' girly with flowers on 'em. Their scent filled the room an' instantly Deja vu shuffled his mind like a deck of cards. He was younger, much younger. At the kitchen table. Sittin' beside her, or on her lap. Davis could hear her laugh faintly as it whispered in an out of the bits and pieces of his memories; it felt like forever ago or yesterday, or maybe not at all, but only a dream. Whatever it was, the smell of the perfume took him there.

Beside them, some framed pictures lay face down on top of a couple ol' shoe boxes Davis knew likely held even more pictures. *Her* pictures. Pictures of them an' the life they'd had before cancer came an' destroyed his childhood like a hurricane. A locked box sat beside it all with a key on top, but Davis knew what was in that one. *My two closest friends*, the ol' man would say. *Smith an' Wesson*. His .357 Magnum. Jus' like everything else in the chest, it'd been a gift from momma before she died, an' one of the earliest

101

memories he had as a kid, learnin' how to shoot with the ol' man. They hadn't been shootin' in years.

He reached down for the first face-down picture frame when the sound of the shed's tin doors closing mumbled outside. As burglar-esk as he'd sneaked-in, Davis rushed back out, careful not to stomp. A trailer snitched on folks runnin' in it like nobody's business. Before the ol' man had half-a-mind to suspect anything, he'd eased the bathroom door shut and turned on the shower. With the scent of his momma's ol' perfume lingerin' in his nose an' the images of Katy's sundress slidin' back into place on his mind, Davis didn't make room to think 'bout why the cedar chest had been out again. The hole in his own chest tol' him wasn't no sense to it anyway.

14

THE SOUND OF SECRETS

TUESDAY

"**M**s. Luanne, where'd you say you had another extension cord?" Davis heard the ol' man ask into the darkness of the house. The porch was nearly done an' he could almost see an end in sight, though he was fairly sure the ol' man would jus' find another job to do somewhere.

She was in there, readin' something. Always was. The uppity ol' lady kept her bird eyes everywhere an' her ears just as open.

"In my hall closet," she replied.

"In the hall closet?" he echoed.

She witch-cackled a laugh. "In the shed next ta the work bench."

"I'll get it!" Allie yelled from somewhere inside, further away.

"I'll give 'er a hand," Davis said eagerly, already sliding his hammer back into the metal rung on his tool belt.

~*~

Davis walked around the porch to the back to help Allie when Ms. Luanne eased out the screen door an' waved a crooked finger toward Mr. Allen.

"Robbie, how come tha' boy a yers don' remember us?" she asked as hushed as a gal like her could manage.

He stammered to respond, but all he could do was sulk his head an' shrug. There'd only been two women his whole life who could make him feel God-awful small with a simple glance of disappointment, and whenever Luanne Quaves joined his wife in heaven, Bob Allen wouldn't know what to do with himself.

"It was...too much, Ms. Luanne. Losin' Mary with all the hospital junk, then the wreck less than a year later. I...I jus'...heavens it was all I could do ta stay workin' an' keep a roof over us. I jus' sorta let go."

Ms. Luanne nodded, knowingly. "When Catfish died, I closed up for a long while, too. Then, when 'em youngin's went an' goofed up an' the church gave us the boot, I's pretty torn up at the thought of what Ol' Catfish might've done or said, too." She shrugged back a few lingerin' lines of wetness as a quiver showed on her lips, but not enough to bring a tear or a break in her firm jaw.

"I'm appreciatin' all yer doin' fer me," she mustered with a wave. "...but I..."

Mr. Allen lifted his hand to halt her words. "Ms. Luanne, you don't need ta say a word. It's a pleasure ta do somethin' fer y'all after all this time. I've felt somethin' awful for all I've done, or ain't done, all these years. This 'ere's the least I could do for you an' yers."

"You ain't ownin' us nothin', Robbie Allen," she said with a half-smirk. "Ol' Catfish'd 'ave you by the scruff o' the neck he 'eard you say somethin' like that."

Mr. Allen laughed, noddin'. "Yeah, but there's a part o' me thinkin' he'd 'ave appreciated me bein' a bigger man all these years, too. One that'd been more involved an' takin' care o' y'all all with these lil' thangs over the years."

Ms. Luanne nodded, understanding, and the sight eased Mr. Allen's conscience a bit. Where he might have been failin', somethin' about Davis' goof-up seemed to be fillin' an old hole o' sorts.

"Does he...," Ms. Luanne started with a point toward where Davis had disappeared around back with Allie, then struggled to find the right words. It wasn't because she's worried 'bout how she might sound or what he might think, he knew, but there was somethin' else there she needed to know, an' the look in her eye tol' him she didn't seem quite sure if she should push it beyond a wonder. "Does he know 'bout *her*? 'Bout Kenny or..."

Mr. Allen shrugged, but then shook his head doubtfully.

"I ain't talked about it," he replied. "Took all the pictures down years back. Couldn't look at 'em. An' now I see'm all growin' up an' lookin' dang near the same an'..."

Ms. Luanne nodded sadly. She thought to say somethin' 'bout how much them bein' 'round was weighin' on Allie, but decided not to. The girl would tighten up her boots for as long as she needed to, she knew. She was tough that way. Always had been. Luanne used ta worry 'bout her grit 'til the first time she saw her take a line drive to the gut, catch it before it could fall, then throw out the runner at third. As if that hadn't struck a nerve with the crowd, she watched as she stepped up lead-off batter an' sent the first pitch over the fence for the game winnin' run. Catfish didn't say a word back then, only patted her leg and smiled.

When the sound of the backdoor screen easin' shut echoed through the darkness of the house behind her, Luanne nodded and patted Mr. Allen on the hand with a wink.

"Aight then," she said. "Y'all get in gear 'fore this 'ere storm front comin' in leaves ya standin' in a puddle."

~*~

They met at the back door. Allie looked tired, exhausted even, but that only made her an eight instead of her normal eleven out of ten. An unexpected smile quickly brought her score beyond any other girl in his class.

"Y'all really ain't gotta do all this, ya know?" she said, swipin' some hair from her face as she led the way to the shed. They'd fixed the fence, the steps, an' nearly the entire porch; replaced missin' sheets of vinyl siding, and Davis still wasn't sure how or why the ol' man insisted they kept going. Didn't he like the idea of a few days off during Spring Break?

"I know. Ol' man won't let me sleep."

"That's Mr. Robbie. Never would let even a lil' thang go without somethin' big in return."

"You sure do know a lot about him, an' remember a lot about me, but why cain't I remember y'all?"

Allie shook her head. Her eyes flicked from Davis, then back to the shed.

"I think you's just a lil' too young, maybe? Back then things were busy, a lot faster than they are now. At least, for me. I remember high school an' how go-go-go everything felt. These friends. Those friends. Concerts. School, work, then ridin' out to the river an' the beach at nights an' on the weekends. Sittin' down without friends 'round felt like dyin' back then. Then you get older Davy, an' havin' a real, true friend is rare. You'll look back an' realize all those folks you thought were your friends were actually jus' sorta there because there was some sort of benefit they got from bein' 'round you. It's when things get tough an' everyone else abandons you, real friends stand up; at least, you hope one does."

They walked in the dark room an' Allie didn't even reach over to turn on the light. When Davis tried it only relented with a deep 'click', but nothing happened.

"It's out," she said. He could see her shake her head from the light of the door. Between her an' the rest of the shed a large tarp covered somethin'. All he could see were muddin' tires peeking out from beneath. Davis glanced back, confused. They parked the Jeep in the garage, not the shed.

"Got a second truck? One for Cruisin'?"

"Uh, somethin' like that," she said. "It's a classic sure 'nough, jus' not that sort. Won't be takin' her out for Cruisin' the Coast, if that's what ya mean." She snatched the coiled cord off the bench and handed it to Davis with a dim smile, suddenly in a hurry to be out of the darkness. In her other hand, she held a tied up grocery bag of somethin' else. Whether she was afraid of the dark or the possibility of critters lurkin' in the dark, he couldn't tell.

When she handed him the rolled cord, she handed him the secon' bag, too. Her mouth opened to say somethin', but only a strangled sigh of somethin' escaped. Whatever it'd been, she'd changed her mind. Davis could only stand and stare at the bag, dumbfounded. It was the bag of crushed beer cans he'd tossed in the ditch the night of the wreck.

"You're better than *this* life, Davy," Allie said. She glanced over her shoulder toward where she guessed his ol' man was in the distance. "You both are..."

His phone buzzed in his pocket an' both of 'em heard it. He checked it. *Dillon.* Allie waved for him to take it, then hurried into a jog back to the house. Davis watched her go, as he slid the phone to his ear.

"Dude, you dead?" Dillon said before Davis could even answer.

"Yep. Leave a message. Beep!"

"What's up? You leave the party, get in a wreck, an' then don't speak for days? You tryin' to get people talkin' on purpose?"

"Ain't a secret, *Sarah!* Quit yer naggin'. Get yer panties out yer crack! The ol' man's been up my butt ev'ry day since the wreck. Where'm I gonna go? He's got me out 'ere fixin' the whole dad-gummed fence an' house. Today's his las' day off though, so..."

"Sounds 'bout right. My ol' man would-a tore me a new one, made me pay for it, an' then had me doin' slave labor too, I guess. That is, if I's stupid 'nough ta get caught!"

Dillon laughed.

"We'll stupid enough ain't *yer* issue. You got tha' covered. Cain't rightly *un-wreck* a truck though."

"I tol' you you had too much to drink."

"No, you tol' me *you* had too much to drink. You even started lookin' at Paige, bro. That's desperate!"

"You'd know."

"I left 'cause I's gettin' tired."

"I tol' you ta stay over, man," he replied, and Davis did remember him offerin' that. Problem was, at least a handful of girls were there and each of 'em had a few too many drinks. If he'd have been there much longer, Davis would've found himself in a hole without a shovel, and at least two or three girls kickin' dirt down on him when the stories started.

"You wanted me to go so you could 'ave a go at Kat," Davis teased.

"Whatever, dude," came Dillon's reply. "How long is the Goblin out?"

"Ain't sure. Ain't heard back yet."

"Tha's rough. Hey, I'm headin' down to the river tomorrow night. Fishin' by day, partyin' at night. I could swing by an' pick you up while the ol' man's out."

"I dunno. Might need to pass it by my ol' man."

"The ol' man? He ain't workin' at all? Wait! You ain't tied up *all break*, are ya?"

"Nah, jus' what I done tol' ya. Workin' like a dog."

"As punishment? You ain't getting' paid, are ya?"

"Hell yeah! I don't work fer free," he lied. *Why did he need to seem tougher for some reason*, he wondered as he looked to the back porch where Allie had entered, but then shook the thought from his mind.

"Jus' tryin' ta save up to fix the Goblin, huh?" Dillon asked.

"Yeah," he lied.

"Well, maybe I could swing by an' help, then we could cut out early?"

"Nah, I don't feel like hearin' you whine about missin' a chance to fish all day while I do all the work."

"Aight, well, ask the ol' man an' let me know. I'd hate to 'ave my pick without you there."

"Tha's the only way you'll get your pick of 'em is if I'm *not* there," Davis replied.

"You sayin' I'm ugly?"

"Well, I ain't sayin' yer not. Maybe you jus' ain't as purdy," he finished with a laugh.

Once he hung up, Davis stared at the bag in his hand and wondered what, if anything, he should do. After all, she'd given it to him, not his ol' man, an' he couldn't help but be both relieved an' worried at the same time. Sure, if she'd given it to the ol' man Davis would be dead, but then there's somethin' else there too, he knew. He'd seen her at the River Lair with Cora Lynn, so that meant she might know 'bout other stuff, too.

~*~

Ms. Luanne eased back down in her chair as Allie finished up in the kitchen then walked back by, picked up her book, and glanced at the clock. There was only about an hour or so before they needed to pick up Kelli.

"Find it okay?" she asked.

"Yes, momma," Allie replied. "Stuff don't wander off too much 'round 'ere."

She smiled. "Well, give me a few minutes an' then I'll get all gussied up so we can go pick up our gal an' get ta our appointments."

Allie nodded as if she hadn't even considered rushing her.

Ms. Luanne watched her walk up the stairs, back to her room, with her thoughts lingerin' on everything from the weather to dinner, an' all them kids an' their knuckleheadedness. But out of all of it, the one thing she couldn't wrap her mind 'round was a few words Robbie had said 'bout how guilty he'd felt, an' how he hadn't been doin' nothin' all these years. She glanced to the letter sittin' on the table, the one they'd cut open jus' this mornin' addressed to them; the one they'd been getting' for almost ten years every month without fail with money in it. It'd been that money that'd helped them through the hard times; kept food on their table when Catfish's pension shifted, and that 'change they *couldn't* believe in' took it's toll on her healthcare bills.

Oh, Lordy, she thought to herself an' the Big Man upstairs, *what've You been up to all these years? An' who You been sendin' to help us in our mess if it ain't been Robbie Allen?*

15

CLOSED DOORS

TUESDAY MORNIN'

The phone rang in the kitchen. Liam hopped up from the rockin' chair an' eased in the screen door an' answered it, leavin' his journal an' bible on the porch.

"Hey you!" the sweet voice on the other end said.

"Hey, Momma," he replied. "How's it goin'?"

"Oh, hot. Busy. You know."

"How's Pop?"

"Out on some routes 'round the villages right now. Clinics. We have a team of eye docs came down with a bunch of ol' prescription lenses. It's a real blessin'," she said. Liam could tell in her voice the chit-chat wasn't what she's hopin' for, an' somethin' else lingered there.

"What's up? You sound flustered."

An odd pause led into her usual "Well…" an' that could only mean one thing.

"Sam called lookin' fer Pop, but since he wasn't here…"

"Okay," Liam said, hopin' his sweet momma would stop dancin' around the tough stuff an' get right to it.

"I-is there anything you wanna say, first?" she asked with a sigh.

A knock on the front door lifted Liam's eyes to Chris's starin' at him through the glass. He waved him around toward the back. The sound of the shower goin' upstairs brought another sigh, but Liam could only do what he knew he ought. He stepped back out onto the back porch and waved for Chris to take his seat, then leaned against the rail beside the grill.

"Yes, ma'am," he finally answered. He didn't want to say everything in front of Chris on the account of sharin' too much of Jewel's personal mess with the world —which was what it felt like, truth be tol'— but it seemed he didn't have too much of a choice. So, with Chris sittin' quietly, the sound of the shower echoin' down the stairs, an' his momma likely sittin' worried as all get-out 'bout her baby boy alone at home with some girl, Liam tol' them both the whole story.

By the time he finished, Chris's Bulldogs' hat rested on his knee an' a frustrated hand wrestled in his hair.

"I, well, don't you think this might look bad to others, Liam?" she asked.

"Course I thought o' that, Momma, but what am I supposed ta do? Let her fend for herself? Say, 'good luck'? She ain't got nothin' or nobody. If it'd been a fella I found on the side o' the road, nobody would've said two words 'bout it."

"I know, but it ain't sweetie. It's a woman. A single woman. An' you're a young handsome man livin' alone."

"Whoever they are, they're gossipin', Momma," Liam replied. "The first night she slept in my bed an' I slept on the couch. Every night since, once I fixed up the spare room, she's slept there. We haven't hid an' I've been honest an' open with everyone. I even called Pastor Sam an' left him a message like Chris an' Terry said I should. He should've called me back, first, before he called y'all."

"I'm glad he called us, Liam," she replied.

"Yeah, but he didn't talk to me, first," Liam said. "Besides, you're busy doin' good work, Momma. You don't need to worry 'bout no foolish gossip. I'm not about to ruin my relationship with God over a girl I jus' met."

"I know, sweetie, but," she sighed. "It's jus', people jus'... Isn't there somewhere else she could stay? What about the older women in the church? Candice or Lauren's house?"

"Momma, Mrs. Candace an' Mrs. Lauren didn't find her. I did. Y'all left me with this big ol' house to look after while I'm goin' ta school. An' here's this girl in need an' I'm supposed ta jus' shove her off on somebody 'cause folks are thinkin' we're doin' something wrong? Is that what Scripture teaches —that when I have what someone needs, I'm supposed to jus' pray for 'em an' send 'em on their way? Y'all taught me a lot better than that. Jus' 'cause folks wanna gossip ain't a good 'nough reason fer me to shy away. Now, if I was tempted or strugglin', that'd be a different story. I'd understand the issue. But it ain't. 'Course, I'll do what you an' Pop decide, and," Liam couldn't help but stare at Chris when he said the next part, "I'll take whatever consequences come my way, if I gotta, but I'm innocent an' I ain't doin' nothin' wrong but showin' Jesus an' bein' a friend to someone who ain't got one."

Liam could tell by the sound of her voice, she knew he wasn't lying, but he could also tell what all this would look like to his Pop as soon as he caught wind of it, too. It'd only be a matter of time before another phone call put Jewels out somewhere. He'd even bet a few more church folks would be called to prod for another place fer her to lay her head before he was done talkin' with Chris.

"Well, Chris is here Momma, an' by the looks of things I think he's here to talk 'bout the same thang."

"Okay, sweetie. I'll be prayin'."

Chris could only stare at Liam, shakin' his head. He knew that look. It said *I gotta do somethin' I don't agree with* an' Liam already knew what it was.

"How's yer Mom an' 'em?" he asked.

"She said hot an' busy."

"Stays hot down 'ere. You remember the rides in the buses, an' when we had to do the roofin' of the orphanage? Like workin' in an armpit."

They shared a sigh at the memory.

"I meant what I tol' Momma, man," Liam said. "I ain't wrong an' I'll put my hand on the bible an' say it all over again, if I thought it'd mean somethin'."

"I'd still be sleepin' without a secon' thought, man," Chris replied. "bible or no bible. Heck," he picked up Liam's journal. "You an' I both know I could jus' as likely read this fella 'ere an' find out the truth of it all, too."

"Yeah, but none o' that matters, huh?"

"Not with these sorts of things, no."

"After all this time, they're jus' gonna assume the wors', huh?"

"There's too many folks who fall for less, buddy," Chris replied. "Ain't all 'em knights like you, bro."

"Lot o' good bein' a knight is if nobody believes you're livin' up to the code."

Liam shook his head. It felt like it was hangin' on by the shoelace, jus' danglin'. What good did it mean to even have character if no one trusted it?

"You've been relieved of all yer positions at the church, buddy," Chris said.

"Fired, huh?" Liam asked as much as said, shakin' his head.

"*Relieved* sounds purdier," Chris replied with a dull grin. Liam knew it bothered him to say so, but he was the director of the youth, young adults, and small groups. It put him in a tough position; one that answered to another authority an' Liam could only imagine the conversation that'd likely taken place before Chris had agreed to drive down an' meet him face to face.

"I ain't never been fired from a job before," Liam replied, shakin' his head.

"Not jus' any job. A *volunteer* job. Takes a special kind of fella ta get fired from a volunteer job. That's Auburn fan material right there," Chris said with a smirk.

Liam shook his head. He couldn't help but grin. Chris could crack jokes on the car ride back from a loved one's funeral visit.

"What would they do if I's a Cowboys fan?" Liam played along.

"You 'eard what the churchy folk did to Jesus back in his day, didn't ya?"

Liam winced. Chris nodded.

"I'm sorry, buddy," he said, suddenly serious. "I have to honor my authority."

"I know, an' I do, too," Liam replied. Chris stood to leave, but Liam wasn't finished. "But I'm not wrong, an' Scripture ain't wrong, neither. God's the real authority here. It's the gossips who need to be hunted out, rebuked, fired, an' given the chance to repent. And he should've called me back an' talked to me 'bout this face to face like a man. I'm twenty-five, not twelve."

Chris nodded, startled a little at Liam's sternness an' the fact that he'd even raised his voice a lil'.

"I appreciate you treatin' me with some dignity, at least," Liam finished.

Chris pointed his finger at Liam. "Only 'cause you ain't a Cowboys fan! If you's Terry," he cut his throat with his thumb then shoved it over his shoulder. "They'd be huntin' fer you down-river."

He grabbed Liam in a bro-hug: three sharp pats to the back followed by a grim nod of manliness.

"Does Terry know?"

Chris shrugged.

"Let's see how long it takes him to find out then."

"He's got a wife an' two kids, bruh," Chris replied. "He'll likely be 'round by lunchtime."

Chris didn't make it to his truck before Jewel appeared in the doorway, a mug of coffee cupped in her hands.

"They doin' you wrong 'cause o' me?"

Liam shook his head.

"Nah," he replied. Deep down he wanted to say 'yeah'. He wanted to growl an' complain 'bout how hard he'd worked to get ta where he was now, an' how unfair it was it could all be snatched away by a few folks an' their lyin' tongues, but he didn't. When he looked at Jewel he knew the las' thing he wanted to do was make her feel like this —any of it, after all she'd been through— was *her* fault.

But she wasn't stupid, either.

"He jus' said you's fired, right?"

"Yeah, but it ain't because o' you," Liam replied. He leaned against the door jamb outside the screen door. "Liars'll lie 'bout anything. Some folks believe 'em, others don't."

"An' they believe them over *you*?"

"Mark Twain said it best when he said, 'It's easier to fool somebody than to convince 'em they've been fooled.'."

"So it's like dat?" she asked. "You jus' finna let dem be fooled?"

"Nah," Liam said. "I'll let 'em know. But that don't mean anything will change when I do."

"What're ya gonna do then? If you's fired from church?"

Liam laughed. "Jus' means I cain't teach the classes. I'll keep goin' an' leave 'em with the hard part of explainin' why I ain't teachin'. An' when college classes start back up next week sounds like I'll 'ave more time ta study. Other than that, ain't much I can do, Miss Jewel."

"You fried, Mr. King!" she said with a grin to match his.

"I'm a southerner, Miss Jewel. Everythang's fried down here."

"They really is doin' you wrong though," she said again, this time a lil' more stirred up than the last. "How can they...I mean...you're like…"

Liam could see the confusion and anger bubbling like a stew startin' to ruminate. An' with Miss Jewel it wouldn't take too long before it'd bubble over the top. He patted the rockin' chair, askin' her to sit. When she finally did with a huff, he sighed but she misunderstood.

"I can leave," she said, suddenly.

"No," he said. "I don't want that. I don't think that's right, an' unless my Pop an' Momma say so, I'm not gonna let what they think make that decision neither. Let 'em think somethin's goin' on an' keep heapin' up lies 'til the cows come home, for all I care."

"Then, what's got you all," she started to ask.

"You!" he blurted. "I don't know how I can help you better. I don't know what you want. If you want to start over here, or if you want to go back to Indy?"

"No," she answered so fast even she seemed surprised. "Indy ain't home no more."

"You sound a lot better than Indy, Miss Jewels."

"You be soundin' a lot better than Harrison, Mr. King."

Liam could only shake his head as memories rushed forward like an unexpected wave.

"No," he said. It was a whisper at first, but then as the thoughts, the sounds, and the guilt continued to pile around him, he couldn't stop the stirrin' of the burnin' in his nose that always came before the tears like lightning before the thunder. "No...this has been a long time comin', I reckon. I dodged the first mistake, now I suppose I'm due for one a bit bigger, even if I ain't done nothin' wrong to deserve this one."

"So, you thank because you did somethin' else wrong before that now you's owed this?"

Liam opened his mouth to respond, but it came as no surprise Jewels was quicker.

"So, you thank I deserved to be raped 'cause I done stole all dem bags o' hot fries from the corner store when I's lil'?"

"I didn't mean..."

"You thank I had it comin' 'roun' to me after all dem fools I played when I's in high school?"

He shook his head, suddenly sweaty again at the thought of being interrogated. It was like waking her up all over again on Sunday.

"I ain't seen a lot of Mississippi, an' what I have is trash compared to you! I cain't imagine you could've ever done anything that..."

"My best friend died because of me," Liam blurted. Even the humidity in the Mississippi gulf air seemed to disappear with the words. Jewel shook her head doubtfully, but Liam had hid the lie for too long and watched Jewels carry her guilt and burden in ways he never had. It reminded him of a book he'd read once, about a woman who'd been caught doing one thing wrong and punished for the rest of her life for it while everyone else in her town treated her horribly and secretly did things wrong all the time.

"But ain't that what Jesus is all 'bout?" Jewels asked, confused. Liam didn't miss the tears swellin' in her golden eyes as they looked up at him. "Ain't that what Tamra an' dem tol' me Sunday? They said I-I could start over, clean, an' forgiven. Now you's sayin' you's owed somethin' for what you did wrong before."

Liam's stomach lurched into his throat an' when he tried to reply he choked. His nose burned an' this time he didn't fight the tears. He could only nod as he held a fist in front of his nose and mouth. He slid down the pole to sit on the concrete, nodding along with the tears as they fell.

She was right. Jesus had forgiven him. And how silly did it sound that he'd allowed his Savior to forgive him, but he hadn't forgiven himself.

16

MAD AT MEMORIES

TUESDAY AFTERNOON

The ol' man seemed shaky, jittery all mornin', then downright sweatier than a stuck pig, an' flush an' flustered even after they'd had a couple ham sammiches and Crawtaters for lunch. Barq's root beers had helped him like they would any good man, or so Davis thought, but by mid-afternoon he seemed the same all over again. Davis hadn't seen him get a call or nothin', but then again, the ol' man didn't need too much ta get stirred up. A drill he'd forgotten to charge the battery on, or not havin' the right size screws for a job had been known to set'm off in the past, but that was also with a few beers in him. Now that he'd thought about it, they hadn't had any at this job. And since they'd pretty much been inseparable since the accident, an' there weren't any in the fridge, Davis couldn't remember seein' the ol' man have one in days. He'd heard that alone could cause a few jitters, but his ol' man didn't seem to be like one of them fellers.

Davis pulled the trashcan down to the ditch an' gathered up all the bags along the road and tossed 'em in, buryin' his with 'em. He'd listened to what Allie said, but he also couldn't figure a good way to break the news to his ol' man; at least, not yet an' certainly not with him all crazy-actin'. There'd be a better time to talk about it later, he hoped.

When Cheesy an' his baby-poop green Chevy eased-in at the end of the gravel drive Davis didn't think too much about it. But when Buckwheat tore out the passenger side door, leavin' it open, an' the ol' man started toward him with a purpose, Davis knew somethin' bad was 'bout ta happen. Davis broke into a run behind the ol' man before Cheesy took the first swing.

The ol' man rocked back, out of the way of the haymaker an' came over-top it with a hard left that put Cheesy on the ground like a sack-o-taters. Buckwheat was there a second later with a haymaker of his own. The ol' man hadn't been as ready for this one. It stumbled him into the hood. He snatched him back an' punched him again with a left as Cheesy started to stand. Buckwheat had him by the collar when a knee to the gut doubled him over an' the ol' man drove into him headfirst like a boxer with his man against the ropes. Cheesy started to dash ahead to tackle him but caught sight of Davis midway. His eyes widened unexpectedly, but it was too late. Davis kicked him in the side of the head an' waited 'til his head bounced off the grill of the truck before he punched him with another hard right.

That's when the shotgun went off. Everything stopped.

Allie cocked it, again. The red shell danced down the porch steps as she rested it on her shoulder and started down. Ms. Luanne stood with her hands on the rail.

"Off my property!" she said evenly.

Allie rocked the shotgun back an' leveled it when Buckwheat started to smirk. The ol' man nodded to Davis an' together they slowly backed away. Cheesy had fallen the secon' time an' was crawlin' back up the front of the Chevy.

"You too, Robert! I appreciate what y'all done here, but I'll 'ave none o' this nonsense!"

"But they," Davis started.

"Shut up, Davy!" Allie said, coldly. "Don't you dare sass my momma! You neither, Mr. Allen. Now get! Or so help me..."

The ol' man nodded without a word and waved for Davis to keep backing away with him toward Pearly.

Buckwheat started forward, but Allie stepped forward to match him, tossin' the stock back into her shoulder.

"You ought ta put tha' thing down, darlin'," he said with a defiant chuckle, darin' her.

"Mister, I got a name an' darlin' ain't it!" Allie replied. "Now unless you're stupider than you look, you ought ta jus' head on out."

"He owes us money!" Cheesy growled, spittin' blood on the gravel. He swiped his lip.

"Chester Higgins, I don't care if he owes you a piggyback ride, you can collect it elsewhere, ya hear? Now, get on!"

"We could jus' call the sheriff on y'all for threatenin' us," Buckwheat replied, with an uplifted hand.

"I'm 'bout ta call y'all an ambulance an' let them sort out what happened when after they get 'ere," Ms. Luanne said with a lifted eyebrow that dared him to challenge her.

The sound of Pearly startin' moved 'em back to their truck.

Davis wanted to say something, apologize even, but Allie wasn't hearin' it. All he could do was glance at her an' hope she could feel it in his expression. When the Chevy pulled out after 'em, his thoughts strayed. He looked to the ol' man, but like the night of the wreck he knew he shouldn't speak. There's somethin' 'bout that look on his face tol' Davis he ought ta jus' wait, watch, an' listen.

The longer they drove, the more reckless Cheesy and Buckwheat got, tryin' ta pass 'em on curves an' ridin' their bumper. After he stopped at the four-way on the corner of Marco's an' Cheesy darted up beside 'em like he's gonna try to speed by and block 'em, the ol' man had finally had enough. Once he passed through the town, he ran the truck into the nearest parkin' lot an' hopped out. Cheesy an' Buckwheat stopped with a screech behind 'em.

"We tol' ya, Bob!"

"I'm out!" the ol' man said.

"Ain't out yet!" Cheesy replied.

"Ain't out 'til we say so!" Buckwheat added.

"Y'all don' shut yer mouths, Imma knock y'all out!" Davis growled. He sounded more nervous than he'd hoped, but they glared at him all the same. If his friends an' coaches had called him anything, it was mouthy.

The back of Pearly an' the front of the Chevy served as enemy lines where they stopped briefly, but the tension was thicker than the humidity.

"This ain't 'bout you, kid!" Buckwheat said with a point not even lookin' at him.

"Hell it ain't!" Davis replied. "Got a problem with my ol' man, you gotta problem with me!"

"This ain't personal, kid. It's jus' business. Yer ol' man owes the boss."

"I don't owe nobody nothin'. Tell Compton that! An' if he wants to chit-chat, tell him to come!"

Cheesy an' Buckwheat snickered. "You know that ain't how this works, Bob. You don't pull some money out tha' wallet o' yers, you'll be wishin' you did."

"Save yer threats for somebody might be scared of ya," he replied.

"You think he'll stop with us?" Cheesy said. His smile widened into such a cruel sight Davis shuddered. "You might whoop us, but Harry an' Big Thornton will jus' be a phone call behind us. An' then somebody else after them. Hell, we gotta whole shop o' folks ready to do whatever the boss wants, especially if it means they get yer spot, too."

Davis could only glance at the ol' man and wonder why he hadn't heard it clearly from the first words. *I'm out.* They should've given it all away; been a hint to the real problem his ol' man had with them an' with his jitteriness all day, but they hadn't. He glanced away when he saw the ol' man's shoulders slump under an unseen weight. There was truth in their words, but more than that. They'd said all this in front of Davis.

A door creaked open behind 'em, an' out walked three men. One started to speak before Davis could gather his thoughts.

"Saw y'all pull up. Weren't sure what the fuss was all about, but we figured it was likely car trouble or a fender bender. We went ahead an' called the sheriff for ya an' got some license plate numbers."

"Y'all ought ta jus' butt out," Cheesy growled.

"Easy, fella!" the man with the Bulldogs' hat interrupted with an' uplifted hand. "Cain't rightly pull up in a church parkin' lot an' think you can jus' get ta arguin' 'bout whatever nonsense y'all are about. Take whatever business ya got an' get on, unless y'all got a mind to get right with Jesus."

"Might not be a bad idea," the older man added. "These fellas got an' issue with you, Bob?"

If Davis didn't know any better, by the look on his ol' man's face, he would've thought all five of 'em were likely to pounce on 'em at any moment. His eyes settled on the third guy who had the least to say, the youngest one. He'd simply shoved his hands in his jeans and looked to the ground and the sight helped Davis breathe a lil' easier, mainly 'cause he knew him.

Well, at least knew *of* him. Everyone Davis' age knew *of* Liam King. And the sight of his holstered muscles made Davis feel a lil' better.

"Yeah, if folks had 'been right with Jesus' a few years back, might not be in this mess to start with, whatcha say Sam?" the ol' man spat.

"Now, Mr. Allen…"

"I said Sam, Chris!" the ol' man interrupted with a point. "Sam knows what I'm sayin', an' so do you, huh *Liam?*"

His voice was pure venom now. Davis wondered if a stiff breeze might knock the wall-of-a-man down.

"Still hidin' behind some wanna-be pastor, huh kid? But y'all ain't wrong *this time!*"

He glared at Cheesy an' Buckwheat.

"I can wait on the Sheriff. How 'bout y'all?"

A wide-eyed, uneasy glance from Cheesy to Buckwheat tol' everyone what the ol' man meant by his words. Whatever he wanted 'out' of, was about to be laying on the parking lot while they watched the deputies tear through the Chevy and put at least two fellas in handcuffs. Though a big part of Davis wanted to know, he breathed a lot easier at the sound of the Chevy doors slam and watched it peel off toward the shop.

No one else had anything to say. The ol' man simply shook his head and got back in Pearly an' Davis followed. But whatever sense he had beforehand must've stayed in the parkin' lot. No matter how mad the ol' man looked, or how confusin' everything had been, Davis had heard jus' 'bout enough of it all.

"A'right," he said with a gruff superiority that came somewhere outta left field. "I ain't a stupid kid. What's all this nonsense about?"

He half-figured the ol' man would come unhinged an' holler, gripe, and grumble, or jus' flat out backhand him an' be done with it. Davis didn't expect the sound of the resigned sigh before the ol' man cleared his throat. His hands still trembled through the nerves, settlin' down after all the fightin' an' whatnot. At least that's what Davis figured.

"How far back you remember, son?"

Davis stammered to respond at first, then shrugged, almost embarrassed.

"Bits an' pieces of momma. A smell 'ere an' there. Pictures in my head like the other day when I saw them trucks in the drive. Folks laughin' 'roun' the kitchen table. Honeysuckles growin' on a patch of lattice by the back door."

He didn't miss the ol' man's smirk at the last one.

"Said she wanted that damned piece o' lattice an' all she did was put that stupid vine on it." He shook his head with a chuckle. "I should've made her four of 'em. You'd've thought by the way I carried on back then she'd asked for the Ladners' boat or somethin'."

He shook his head, obviously disappointed at himself in hindsight.

"Son, the long an' short of it is this," he said, wrenchin' the steerin' wheel in his hands like he might tear off the rubber to the metal. "When she died, I did too. An' I don't mean that in some sappy, namby pamby sorta way. I quit. Hell, I still ain't...uh...*un*-quit. I took all the pictures down in the house. I even sent you off to live with yer uncle in Colorado for a spell. I couldn't do life. Nothin' made sense. Only workin' made sense, an' when I got done with that, I'd drink. Then, if I could numb the pain of it all quick enough, I'd hit the bed an' do it all over again the next day. I worked seven days a week for maybe a year."

"But what about all that?" Davis said, thumbin' over his should back down the road. "You said you were 'out', Pop. I know what 'out' means."

The ol' man nodded somberly. "Wasn't too long before the boss called me in to the office an' said he had an idea. He started pokin' around at some lil' jokes here an' there 'bout how we could really pull in some money —*how we could turn some money as easily as we turn wrenches*, he'd said. Then, one day all those jokes and idears jus' sorta fell together an' slowly became more an' more real. Next thang I knew, we's doin' it."

"Doin'..."

"Runnin' drugs," he admitted, shakin' his head with disgust. "Started small. One day a week. One drop. Got some extra tool boxes an' hid the stuff in the lower level. Acted like we's doin' service calls, then we'd fake a repair an' swap out tool kits. Over time the business grew an' so did our lil' operation. Soon, we's sendin' one fella out on services daily. Sure, he'd turn a wrench at three or four stops, but then there's always one he'd do a drop at, too."

"Got us outta the hole what with all yer momma's medical bills, an' regular bills, then some repairs an' whatnot. Then, I's able to buy some more tools 'ere an' there, an' even ease away from bein' on the service runs. Built us a crew of lackeys, some of 'em druggies who couldn't pay up."

"How long have you..."

"'Bout five years."

"When d'ya say you wanted out? Why now?"

"Guess yer wreck sorta woke me up. Reminded me there's more to be missin' again. With yer momma I was sad an' lost. When yer brother got in his accident, I got mad an' angry at everything an' everyone. But with you... Guess I jus' got tired of livin' this way after all this time, an' I felt like I's seein' it come 'round again like a circle. The runnin' an' the sneakin' jus' takes a toll on ya. It weighs on a man... 'specially a man who knows better."

Davis shrugged. "Everybody knows better, Pop. Jus' ain't very many *do* better."

"Those are wiser words than you know, Davy. So, that's the real reason why I ain't bought any more pee-juice an' why Cheesy an' Buckwheat been comin' over more often wantin' to 'talk shop'. I finally tol' Compton I's out, an' I jus' wanted to get back to turnin' a wrench an' nothin' more. At first, he'd agreed, but now I think he's gettin' a lil' uneasy at the thought of somebody bein' 'round but not doin' the dirty work. I mean, if ya ain't in the mix of the mess to them, then yer more likely to rat everyone else out."

"They think after all this time yer jus' gonna toss 'em under the bus?"

The ol' man nodded. "I think it's got their panties all in a wad, an' now they're flexin' to get me back jus' to keep from bein' worried."

"An' they ain't gonna leave you alone?" Davis asked.

"I really don't owe 'em anything. All my debts were paid back long ago, an' any money I owed Compton for unpaid rent an' lil' thangs 'ere an' there I've paid over an' above throughout the years."

"What were ya doin' when you's goin' through the shed the other night after they left?" Davis asked, skeptically.

When the ol' man didn't reply instantly, Davis wondered if he was scramblin' to think up a lie. The truck eased into the drive an' came to a stop. He slipped it up into park, then turned the key. "Had an' ol' box I've been hidin' for a lil' while now. One with lil' keepsake stuff in it. Stuff that'd belonged to yer momma an' yer brother. I's tryin' ta find 'em ta make sure you got 'em jus' in case..." he let the rest of the words disappear with a wave of his hand.

"Do ya think they'd..."

His eyebrows lifted up skeptically, an' they said everything Davis needed him to say. It was one of those expressions that said '*They're likely to do anything.*'

"Well, if they ain't gonna let ya out, what's yer plan?"

The ol' man shrugged. "You oughta not worry 'bout this mess, son. You've gotta lot of..."

"Pop!" Davis said, stealin' his attention. "We're all we've got left. If we ain't in this together, we lose everything. I ain't sayin' I'm worried, but havin' a good plan is like havin' a good glove."

"Aight," he agreed after a few breaths of silence in the cab of Pearly. "On the account they don' let this 'ere thang ride out, an' I cain't talk any sense into these fellers, let's make us up a plan, but I'm gonna see it through, not you. You keep yer nose down an' let me fix this, aight?"

"Yessir," Davis agreed, reluctantly, but he meant it. "It's all yers."

17

TRAVELIN' TOO FAST

TUESDAY EVENIN'

I'm a lil' busy today, Liam. Can we talk about this tomorrow sometime?"

"No sir," Liam replied, and the response forced Pastor Sam to look up from the letter he was reading. "No sir," he said again, this time a bit slower and more emphatic.

"I can understand your confusion in this, but once the board heard about this, my phone didn't stop ringin' with questions."

"Why didn't you return my call?" Liam replied. "All this would-a been sorted out if you'd 'ave returned my call."

"No, I'm afraid it wouldn't have," he replied. "Before you left Sunday, chatter about who tha' nice lil' girl was gettin' baptized echoed around the sanctuary, an' with every unanswered question came another one."

"Sir, I'm not seein' how their mutterin' suddenly makes me a bad man,"

Chris sat silently in the chair. Both men glanced at him, hopin' he'd chime in here an' there. When he didn't, Liam knew he likely wouldn't, an' while that might be okay with him, it likely wasn't okay with Pastor Sam.

"It's not that it makes you a bad man, Liam. It's that it ruins yer witness."

"I keep hearin' that phrase used Pastor, but I don't read that anywhere in scripture. Where did it ruin Jesus' witness to have his feet washed by the prostitute or keep company with sinners and tax-collectors?"

"You ain't Jesus, son," Pastor Sam snickered.

"That ain't scripture, Sir, an' you still didn't answer my question."

"We don't 'ave time to debate this. An' I don't like yer tone. In fact, it ain't up fer debate. The decision's been made, an' it's final."

"Quotin' scripture ain't debate, Sir. An', to be honest, I'm here 'cause gossip is wrong. I got scripture on that."

"Folks bein' concerned about ya is far from gossip, son," Pastor Sam said with an exasperated sigh an' a slight snicker.

"It is when what they're pretendin' to be concerned about ain't true, an' ain't no one askin' me 'bout any of it one way or another. In fact, as far as I'm understandin', that's the textbook definition of a gossip. What's the purpose of building character if someone can slander another person an' dismiss it without anyone blinkin' an eye at the character? Shouldn't I've at least been given the benefit of the doubt here?"

Pastor Sam took in another sigh of finality, glanced at Chris, then back to Liam.

"I think we're done here,"

"We *can* be," Liam replied with a nod, "But I still think it's a shame a man like you don't wanna sort this out with

with scripture. See, you'll refuse to use scripture with someone falsely accused of sin on the account it's only one faithful tither who you know won't leave, over correctin' a dozen or so for gossipin' or slander who'll leave at the drop of a hat."

"Liam," Chris breathed, shufflin' uneasily in his chair. His eyebrows were raised, concerned. Liam knew he might've crossed the line takin' a stab at Pastor Sam's character, but that didn't make the truth any less true. An' if his character could be falsely accused an' ran through the mud behind his back, at least Liam did him an' honor in sayin' so to his face. A dozen older gossips likely paid a hefty amount of the tithes, an' the weight of makin' those sorts of decisions weren't likely easy ones when the pastor's own livelihood depended on that money to survive. That was often the compromise with western pastors, Liam's dad had said more than once. Pastors everywhere wrestled with decisions like these every day. It seemed there were more and more so-called Christians who were willing to be talked to as long as the seats were comfortable, the coffee was warm, and the lessons were encouraging, but not as many who wanted someone to actually pastor or lead them. To them, they could just as easily fill a seat somewhere else next Sunday. To them, it wasn't about the relationship with Jesus or the community of believers, it was self-centered. And sadly, the pastors had allowed them get that way.

"Now you listen 'ere, Liam! I'll not debate this any longer!"

"You won't debate it at all!" Liam growled louder than he could recall ever replying to anyone. Pastor Sam stopped and swallowed hard at the sudden outburst, startled. In the brief silence, Liam waved his hand to say he was done an' nodded. "They're wrong," he mumbled. "You're *all* wrong. All I'm doin' is helpin' this poor girl, and Jesus knows."

Chris stood when Liam turned for the door an' walked him out in silence. They stopped in the foyer when Pastor Sam sped up to them, wide-eyed.

What would he say? Had he considered his words?

"Did y'all see the trucks jus' pull in the lot?" he said. "They look 'bout ready to fight."

He pushed past them to get a better view out the window. "Oh Lord, I know those trucks," he said. "Call it in, Chris. Nothin' good's comin' from this one."

When they stepped out a minute later, the tension in the air was thicker than the humidity. There could be no mistakin' this for coincidence, Liam knew. His meetin' with Pastor Sam had been about Jewel, an' the same two trucks seemed to be starin' back at him like they did on Saturday night, an' the thought stirred his gut. At the sight of Mr. Allen, Liam could only shove his hands deep in his jeans and look away. He'd have given anything to be anywhere else at that moment, but something told him that, as usual, God wasn't workin' with coincidences.

Chris smiled, liftin' up his phone.

"Saw y'all pull up. Weren't sure what the fuss was all about, but we figured it was likely car trouble or a fender bender. We went ahead an' called the sheriff for ya an' got some license plate numbers."

"Y'all ought ta jus' butt out," one man started to complain.

"Easy, Sir!" Chris replied. "Cain't rightly pull up in a church parkin' lot an' think you can jus' get ta arguin' 'bout whatever nonsense y'all are about. Take whatever business ya got an' get on, unless y'all got a mind to get right with Jesus."

"Might not be a bad idea," Pastor Sam added. "These fellas got an' issue with you, Bob?"

Mr. Allen scanned them with a laser in his eyes, an' Liam felt it rest on him.

"Yeah, if folks had 'been right with Jesus' a few years back, might not be in this mess to start with, whatcha say Sam?" Mr. Allen replied.

Pastor Sam didn't respond to the prod, but he didn't need to.

Liam choked. He saw the night all over again, all those years ago, and felt the shame. The worse part was how right Mr. Allen was considerin' all that'd transpired. With his most recent thoughts weighing on him, 'bout a man's character bein' dumped in a ditch without a second glance, he felt the ache of Mr. Allen's spiritual scar as if it had been his own. And in a way, it had been. Sure, everyone had choices to make, but Liam's had led to them all.

One little choice.

One big mistake.

"Now, Mr. Allen..." Chris tried to interject.

"I said Sam, Chris!" Mr. Allen growled with a point. "Sam knows what I'm sayin', an' so do you, huh *Liam?*"

Liam saw the flash of the headlights from the cars on the sand. He was there, again. He heard the laughs of his high school buddies tauntin' him, the pastor's son, about how lame it must be to be 'good' all the time. One party wouldn't hurt. After all, everyone else on the baseball team would be there and so would she. He could still see Allie's pleading eyes begging him to come, too. How could he say no? After all, this was the night she was gonna tell Kenny an' what sort of friend would he be to them if he wasn't there to help 'em through it, even though he'd wished with everything inside him he didn't have to.

"I'm pregnant, Kenny," she'd said.

Liam watched as she stood scared and Kenny could only glance dumbly back and forth between 'em, shakin' his head. Had it been the alcohol, the shock, or fear, Liam didn't know.

Allie fought viciously to keep the tears at bay. She never liked to look weak.

"Say somethin', man," Liam added with a wave to Allie as if she deserved somethin', anything but silence. It wasn't that Kenny didn't love her, he did. It was that he'd lost his mom not even a year before, an' to make matters worse his dad had all but fallen away from everything, leavin' lil' Davy with an' uncle, and Kenny to fend for himself.

Liam had lost count how many times he'd slept in the spare bedroom.

Now, this...

With another glance to Allie's tears pleadin' helplessly, Kenny stretched out a hand to Liam.

"Gimme my keys, bro..."

"What?" Liam couldn't believe his ears. *That's all he had to say?*

"Gimme my keys, Liam!" Kenny growled.

"Come on, man!"

"The *keys!*"

"No!" Liam replied. Kenny shoved him. He looked at Allie. She swiped the tears away like mosquitoes, quick to dismiss 'em with all the people around. What'd started as somethin' small turned the heads of more than a few people on the sand by the river when Kenny shoved Liam.

"*No?* It's *my* truck!"

"Not tonight it ain't."

"Not tonight..." Kenny laughed. "Gimme the keys or I'll beat you down an' take 'em."

"Nah, but...," Liam tried to play it off.

Kenny punched him. Allie rushed forward, but a wild hand shoved her back. Liam wheeled around in time to catch another punch. But when he saw Allie stumble away, he'd thought Kenny hit her. Something snapped.

"Gimme the keys!" Kenny growled, but it was too late.

Liam wrapped his arms around Kenny's waist, lifted him into the air, and slammed him to the sand. He lost count of the punches. More than a few of their teammates rushed to pull Liam away. Allie stood, dumbfounded. It'd all happened so fast.

"Liam!" she screamed. "Don't! Stop! I'm okay!"

"Aight, aight!" Liam said over an' over again to the guys wrestling him away. "I'm good. I'm done." He glanced at Allie, but she looked away an' Liam knew why. He hadn't lashed out at Kenny for hittin' him, an' she knew that. There was only one reason he'd punched him back, an' Allie didn't want Kenny or anyone else to know the truth.

Kenny stirred on the sand, slow at first, then with a jolt of adrenaline, quick to look as strong and confident as ever.

Liam knew better. He knew behind the facades. Kenny was like a brother.

Allie tried to grab his arm, but Kenny wasn't havin' it. He was likely mad he'd shoved her in the first place, but that was the Kenny all three of 'em knew. He'd never admit it 'til they were away from the crowds. It was the way of his ol' man. The same ol' man starin' down Liam as pieces of the memory all those years ago faded back to the vault in Liam's mind an' he found himself again standin' on the steps of the church.

The same steps he'd found himself standin' on a week later when all the families met to decide on how they were gonna respond to the news of Allie's unexpected pregnancy once the word got out.

"Still hidin' behind some wanna-be pastor, huh kid?" he heard Mr. Allen taunt. "But y'all ain't wrong *this time!*"

This time... The words trickled down to his heart and gut where everything jumbled together into a lump that rushed back to his throat. They'd treated the Allens –a family who'd been hurtin' in so many ways for a year since Mrs. Allen passed– like roadkill, an' then dismissed the Quaves family without so much as a wave, too. Good people done wrong.

One little choice.

One big mistake.

A few more words sent the two fellas in the sick green Chevy hollerin' out the parkin' lot, an' Mr. Allen an' Davy weren't far behind. Liam had often wondered if Mr. Allen still held a grudge after years of avoidin' him. Guess bein' in the church parkin' lot all over again had a way of reopenin' old wounds.

Liam had tried to speak during the meetings, but glares from Kenny an' the thought of disappointin' Allie kept him silent. In the end, he watched as his friends' families faced the shame of bein' asked to leave to avoid any more controversy.

"Ain't no sense in you getting' in trouble, too," they'd said. "This was our choice. You knowin' about us an' not tellin' folks ain't what the real problem was in their eyes anyhow."

"It's not about bein' a tattletale, it's about bein' yer friend takin' blame alongside ya," Liam had tried to argue, but they weren't hearin' it. That's how they'd always been with Liam, even though they were only a year older. It was something that came with the territory of bein' the good friend –the protection when times got tough.

"There's no need for you to be punished, too," Allie an' Kenny had said more than once as the days turned to weeks.

Then, the night of the accident changed everything.

When Mr. Allen heard the news, all he could think to say —everything that fueled his guilt and blame— pointed back to that day. Where would they've been had the church not turned its back on them? And at every turn somehow Liam's role seemed to evade all the scrutinizing fingertips an' accusations. After all, he'd been the pastor's son. He alone knew about how serious their relationship had become; about the parties and the way Kenny had slipped away from Jesus an' into the alcohol like his ol' man, an' to make matters worse Liam had even been at some of the parties. Sure, he hadn't had more than a sip here an' there —beer was disgusting— but that was beside the point. What nagged at Liam was how much more of a friend he could've been to Kenny by standin' in his path like he did that night on the river's edge. At the time, all he could think about was what would happen if he did. To stand in their way meant to lose him.

An' when he didn't, he still lost him.

18

COLLISION

TUESDAY EVENIN'

Jewel was on the phone when Liam walked in with Chris. The sight took him by surprise. She hadn't even shown any interest in usin' the phone. He wasn't even sure she knew anyone's number to call.

Liam pointed toward the fridge an' Chris nodded. Two cold Barq's root beers clinked together as they stood on the back porch less than a minute later.

"Well, that went over 'bout as well as a fart durin' prayer, wouldn't ya say?" Chris said.

Liam shook his head with a laugh. Only someone raised in church could appreciate a good joke like that. He smirked, but he was sure Chris could see the reluctance there, too. He hadn't handled himself as coolly as he'd wanted. The injustice and dishonor of it all weighed on him a lil' more than he cared to admit. Liam's mind hadn't really been on that part of the evenin' as much as the standoff in the parkin' lot had, but now with them walkin' back into the room with Jewel things started to shift, an' the reality of it all sorta settled back to the unpleasant *present*.

Didn't take 'em too long eavesdroppin' through the screen door to figure out who's on the other end of the line. Only one gal could talk with three folks an' be the only one in the conversation.

"Angel says Hi, an' to pick up some bread on the way home," Jewel relayed once she finally got off the phone. "Looks like I'm busy with the girls all day tomorrow."

"Better you than me," Chris mumbled.

"Good," Liam said. "That ought to be fun."

"Think so?" Uplifted eyebrows showed her skepticism. "Said Tamra has plans an' that we're doin' some kinda study tomorrow too."

"Wednesday night bible study," Chris inserted with another long drawl on his root beer.

"Every Wednesday," Liam added. "Seven to eight-thirty or so. Wow, you really *will* have a full day tomorrow then, huh?"

Big eyes pleaded with Liam to reassure her in some way.

"It really will be fun. It'll be good fer ya to get outta here an' away from me a lil' too."

"What about you? Where you finna be? Not church..."

"Got 'em...," Chris replied with a smirk, then shook his head somberly and sipped his root beer.

"At the park. Mr. Montgomery needs me on as many shifts this week as I can offer. Actually, I need to get goin' soon, if I'm gonna make it down there in time for tonight."

"Take yer time, bro. I'll give you a ride."

"In Spring Break traffic?"

"Okay, well, half-way...," he replied with a wince.

~*~

"Allens, huh?" Mr. Montgomery shook his head an' his expression showed what he meant.

"An' on the same day I'm talkin' with pastor about Jewel no less."

"Ain't much of a coincidence neither, is it?"

"God ain't much for 'em," Liam replied. "I'm thinkin' that's the only solid part of all this that's makin' it bearable —knowin' at least He's knowin' what's goin' on even if I don't."

"Bein' able to have half a mind about ya ought to be proof enough. Neither me nor Sam had those sorts of thoughts at yer age, that's fer sure."

"Can I ask you somethin'?"

Mr. Montgomery's eyes flicked from the line outside the roller coaster to Liam with a dubious look as if to say that'd been a stupid question. "'Course, kiddo. Shoot!"

"What d'ya do when you suddenly realize you've been livin' with somethin' an' ya been lettin' the world move on aroun' ya, but you ain't forgiven yourself? How'd...how can I..." Liam's lips kept movin', but no more words seemed to be comin'.

Mr. Montgomery nodded with a resigned sigh-of-a-sound, like he understood all too well.

"Most folks never ask that question, 'cause they think others'll judge 'em for not knowin'. Truth is, it ain't easy. Sure, folks can sound all biblical and theological an' make you feel small answerin' all scriptural 'bout it like its easy, but it ain't. I think that's why Jesus talked so long about it, an' then Paul, Peter, an' John carried on about it as much as they did in their letters to the churches. Forgiveness is tough. An' if we're our harshest critics, then I'd say forgivin' ourselves is likely one of the hardest things to do, too. Sure, we can say it, an' pray it, but can we live it out? Like I always say..."

"Well done is better than well said," Liam finished.

Mr. Montgomery lifted a finger with a wink. "You got it."

"Mr. Montgomery?" one of the newbies interrupted. "We've got a couple of guys tryin' ta pay with a card inside, but they say they don't have I.D."

"I'll take it," Liam said. Truth was, he needed a break from the conversation. After all that'd happened, Liam couldn't wait to simply close his eyes an' be done with the day. It'd been a long time since he'd felt that way, but nothin' had seemed clear or easy since Saturday night, an' the past three days had felt more like three months.

He took the card from the newbie an' smirked at the guy waitin' at the counter.

"Sorry 'bout all this," he said. "These card readers are somethin' else. Did Tim ask for I.D.? We might jus' be able to put the charge in manually, Mr...." Liam looked at the card.

Jewel Slayton.

He stopped an' looked up slowly.

"J`well," the skinny man corrected. "All y'all be tryin' ta call ya boy Jewel, like I'mma female or somethin'. It's J`well."

Liam choked for a second, then faked a smile. "It ain't nothin', Mr. *J`well.* I can have it send a message to your phone. D'ya got the phone linked to the card?"

"Naw! It got stolen. Folks be finessin' out here."

"Okay," Liam replied. He pretended to be workin' with the computer, tryin' to sort his thoughts out an' cool off as his mind swam an' his imagination started-in.

This is one of the guys! It screamed. *You don't know that! He could've got it from someone else...or found it.*

Liam slid it into the crack on the drawer beneath the machine, pretending to insert it into the card reader.

Hmm, he sounded. He winced. "Man, I'm sorry 'bout yer wait. Why don't ya have a few rides on the house while we try an' get this figured out. I'll have a chat with the manager an' see what we can do, Mr. J`well."

"Free rides?"

"Yessir. Tell'em Liam sent ya," he replied. "It's the least we can do..."

"Aight!" He turned around and nodded to a bigger man near the pool tables, who nodded an' then threw his arm aroun' the shoulder of a girl.

As they went out the game doors to the park, Liam told the newbie to watch the desk an' walked out front into the small parking lot. It didn't take him long to spot the car.

"Gotcha!" he mumbled. He jotted down the license plate number, walked back inside, an' called the cops. Before they even finished wreckin' the tires encircling the fast track of the Go-karts, the Sheriff's department had arrived. Liam watched 'em search the car from a distance an' asked a deputy if he could look through some of the stolen bags that'd been jammed in the trunk. From the looks of things they'd been doin' the same routine every night. Liam shuttered at the thought of how many girls like Jewel were out there, an' how they might be copin' without a friend. Maybe they had friends or family, he considered, but then tossed the thought aside. He said a quick prayer for 'em, an' for the two guys —that they'd know Jesus, or at least learn somethin' 'bout 'em while they're servin' their deserved jail time. All the stolen purses in the trunk an' even a few bags of drugs to fill-in the rest of the date rape drama helped the cuffs on a lil' easier.

"Well, how 'bout that!" Mr. Montgomery said once the police pulled out of the parking lot an' the tow truck removed the car. "Looks like a good endin' to a rough day, if ya ask me."

"I'll take the silver linin'," Liam replied with a grin.

"Wanna head on out an' tell our gal?" he added with a pat. Liam thought to dismiss the offer, what with the crowd an' all, but it seemed like there were enough newbies to keep things under wraps. Besides, Mr. Montgomery knew how to manage an' he likely wouldn't have offered if he hadn't thought 'bout it.

He nodded.

"Jus' gimme a call when you make it, aight?"

"Sure thing. An' whenever my buddy gets here later, tell em' I'm gonna come visit with him tomorrow before work."

"Sitter ought ta have him down at the river 'roun' lunchtime, oak side. You could peek in an' surprise him," Mr. Montgomery offered with a hapless shrug.

"Aight," Liam replied. "Might jus' do that."

~*~

Once Liam got home an' shared the news of the men at the Park an' handed Jewel what was left of her things they'd found in the trunk of the car, he thought she'd be a lil' more excited than she was. Not that he'd hoped for some gushin' thanks or anything, but she jus' sort of stared at 'em layin' there on the counter like she's scared to touch 'em. Right then he realized there were likely other thoughts lingerin' there too, ones he really didn't understand.

Ones he didn't want to.

In a way, he'd sort of hoped with all that'd gone on with him recently –seein' Mr. Allen again– this could be a sort of closure an' justice he felt he's missin' in his own life. But she'd jus' stood there, starin' at her things with a numb caution, her eyes wanderin' somewhere else altogether. Had it been more of a reminder, again, of somethin' bad from the past? She didn't say for certain. Liam might not know a lot about what she'd been through, but he certainly understood that relivin' the past was far from pleasant. Before she went to bed, Jewels slowly perused through the bag, but finally closed it back an' shoved it away. He wanted to ask her more than one question, but decided to write them in his journal instead. Some things were better left unsaid.

WEDNESDAY MORNING

When he opened his eyes the bed felt surreal, like it was there, but not. Almost like he's floatin' on it, or in it, but that it might fall out from under him at any time an' there wouldn't be too much he could rightly do 'bout it if it did.

A lotta things had been feelin' that way lately.

It was warm half-under the sheets, invitin', but still a lingerin' chill bit at his toes, remindin' him that though a bed might feel warm from time to time, not havin' someone to share it with kept it jus' a tad off, never quite warm enough. The past few days had been more than he'd imagined, a lil' bit too much to take in, but then again, he'd asked for it, hoped for it even.

Let's go back, he'd heard the voice, or was it a thought? He wasn't sure.

After that night everything went haywire, up, down, an' every which way. What it all meant he couldn't tell, but there's a big part of him wondered if he even ought ta try an' make heads or tails of it all. Things sorta jus' panned out after a while when a fella finally stopped strugglin' with things, didn't they? He knew a lotta folks messed up more than one good thing simply overthinkin' it, an' rushin' 'ere an' there without a lick-o-sense. He didn't wanna do that. Not if this was his only chance to get back to something good.

But what if he couldn't —get back? What if there weren't no gettin' back to good?

Don't think like that, he heard again in the stillness of the early mornin'. In the back of his mind he heard the familiar sound of somethin' turnin, grindin' its way to move, pushin' through the years of muck an' grime to fight free like a gear needin' more grease.

I'll take you back, the voice came again, like it had on that night —what seemed like a year ago, but had only been a few days.

Keep movin'! We'll get there.

19

SPARE PARTS

WEDNESDAY MORNING

"So, what're we doin?" Dillon asked, again. It was clear his mind was twelve hours ahead with his toes in the sand, a drink in his hand, an' a girl under his arm. Anything else jus' seemed like a waste of his focus. The ol' dirt road wasn't far, 'bout twenty yards from the back fence. Davis pointed to a small pull-off where they often avoided some of the bigger dips when they were muddin' an' Dillon pulled his truck to the side.

"Swingin' by to check on the Goblin," Davis replied. He wanted to throw a good mouthy stab in there, too. Somethin' 'bout how many times he'd said it already, or if he needed Helen Keller to translate or somethin', but he could tell Dillon's askin' probably reflected his reluctance more than anything.

It *was* true. Davis *did* hope his truck was bein' repaired by a few of the other mechanics who knew his ol' man a bit better than to run him through the mud 'cause he wanted somethin' better for his family, but a bigger part of him

149

knew those hopes had vanished with his ol' man's allegiance. Now, the only thoughts scurryin' 'roun' his mind were if and how he could sneak his truck out of harm's way before the whole mess got messier.

"An' yer sure this is a good idea?" Dillon asked.

"Nope," he admitted.

"Man, I really ain't a fan of yer honesty sometimes. Still cain't believe them two did that," Dillon said, shakin' his head. He'd told him what happened at the house an' the fight, but he'd left out a few choice bits he didn't figure was his business – mainly all the junk 'bout the drugs an' his ol' man. If everything turned out the way him an' his ol' man had planned, the less everyone else knew the better. Folks in Harrison weren't the best at lettin' old mistakes roll on.

Dillon tossed his truck in park an' nodded.

"If they do you wrong on purpose they'd lose their jobs, don't ya figure?"

Nope, Davis knew with surety, but didn't say. He shrugged as if Dillon had a point, then opened the door. His bud's optimism would only help him for so long, so Davis knew he'd need to hurry up an' test the waters before his gumption snapped away like a fishin' line. If Dillon started gettin' too worried, everything would turn to crap. Two guys stood out back, smokin'. They waited 'til they flicked the butts away an' got back to work before they pushed their luck aroun' the openin' in the fence an' through the overgrown back lot where all the abandoned ones had been collectin' rust. The entrance to the lot was clear on the other side, away from the woods, but they'd have needed to drive past more than one set of large glass windows in clear view of everyone, an' would've been met by folks before the truck stopped. At least this way Davis hoped he could see the

Goblin an' at best grab the rest of the paperwork out of the dash.

Halfway through the lot, walkin' like them folks walk at the mall in the mornin', they caught sight of the unmistakable green paint job an' his heart sank a lil' more. The Goblin sat jus' as rough as it'd been when Mr. Tommy loaded it on the back of the tow truck. Eyes fixed between the shop door an' the Goblin, he'd forgotten altogether about the cages. Next to seein' Mr. Compton himself, the thought of the two Rottweilers, Tango and Cash, gettin' after 'em were enough to make him squirm. When they started-in barkin', Dillon nearly leapt a foot in the air, an' suddenly Davis's pessimistic *nope* earlier seemed a lot more definite in both their minds.

How Davis could ever forget about them after all the stories he'd heard from his ol' man he wasn't sure, but the desire he saw in their eyes to kill, spittle dribblin' from their lips, settled any dispute firmly into place.

Before they could decide whether to run for it or not, the back door creaked open an' scraped across the concrete.

"What're y'all doin' back here?" a guy Davis didn't know asked.

"I... we's jus'..." Davis started to explain pointing from the drive aroun' to the car lot. "Thought we could take a peek an' see if y'all'd started on her or not. Startin' school again next week, an' baseball season's comin' up. Eager to get 'er back."

If the man sympathized, he didn't show it.

"Ain't sure how you got 'roun' here, but you'd better get yer hind end's back out!"

Another man crept out from the darkness an' his eyes lit up at the sight of Davis.

"Hey boy!"

151

"Whatcha say, Mr. Cliff?"

The new guy glanced between 'em.

"Allen's boy," Mr. Cliff explained, thumbin' toward Davis.

Maybe Davis was readin' into it a lil' too much, but at the mention of his ol' man he thought he saw something turn-on like a light switch in the new fella's eyes. It reminded him of football –the look the offense brought up to the line knowin' what the play was gonna be.

The newbie disappeared back inside without a word. Mr. Cliff wiped his hands on his shop rag. "Not too much, punk." He nodded toward the Goblin. "How'd ya bust 'er up?"

"Turns out yer supposed ta keep it between the ditches?" Davis joked.

"No kiddin'! Well, hot dog. Learnt that'n the hard way, didn't ya?"

"Expensive way," Davis said with a laugh. "Well, that's what I was aimin' ta see," he said with a point. "I's hopin' ta get her back sooner, with school startin' an' all, but..."

Mr. Cliff winced, noddin' along, then glanced to the door. The expression on his face said it all. *The newbie'd be back soon. Davis oughta scram.*

"It's good seein' ya, Sir." Davis said a lil' too hurriedly than he'd wanted it to sound, but the old man simply grinned.

"Shame what's goin' on. Tell yer ol' man I said hey."

"Yessir. Sure thing."

Davis an' Dillon started away when the door scraped open, again.

"Hey, hold up you two," the newbie said. "Boss says he wants ta see ya."

~*~

Mr. Compton stayed at his desk, didn't even look up when the newbie pointed them towards the door.

"Heard y'all's snoopin' 'roun' back?"

"They call it snoopin' if I'm lookin' at *my* truck?" Davis replied. "We's in the area an' stopped by to see if she might be close to..."

"Could've sicked 'em dogs on ya," he said, an' Davis believed him. He'd heard more than one story 'bout thieves Tango an' Cash had dealt with that'd made his skin crawl.

"Glad ya didn't. I'm purdy sure they would've gotten sick chompin' on him." Davis replied thumbin' toward Dillon with a fake laugh. In all his life, he'd never known Mr. Compton to crack more than a small sideways grin. So, when he saw that, he felt at least a lil' relieved.

"D'ya think I didn't hear about the fight or somethin'?"

"Two half-drunk eijets ramblin' about somebody owin' somebody money? That's got somethin' to do with *my* truck?"

"Half-drunk, huh?"

"Well, I figured they must've been, thinkin' they could jus' pull up at my job an' pick a fight. That or stupid. But now that ya mention it..."

Mr. Compton cracked a smirk again.

"I like you kid, always have. So, I'll let this slide, but tell yer ol' man this 'ere truck might turn up missin' if he don't pay me a visit himself," Mr. Compton said without so much as liftin' his face from the paperwork on the desk.

Davis thought to threaten him if he did, but the gruff tone of the old man's voice reminded him of a movie villain. He was cold and calculated, a sorta fella who knew the ins an' outs of things with the surety of a skilled craftsman –the mechanic with a comfortable engine, or a carpenter choosing wood to work. In life, there were two types of people: those who pretended to be tough 'cause they'd watched too many movies, an' those the writers of those movies likely created 'cause there were folks out there somewhere who existed jus' as scary as the ones they were tryin' ta create. Right then, with all he now knew, every ounce of Davis screamed Mr. Compton was the secon' one, an' he didn't feel like lingerin' 'roun' or smartin' back to find out.

Besides, he hadn't had a fear in the world of sayin' any of it in front of Dillon, either. The same Dillon whose eyes looked wider than baseballs when they walked out the shop an' pretended they'd walked down the road. It'd be a long walk around the woods, but it was worth sellin' that they hadn't been snoopin'. Jus' like his ol' man had said, there were old toolboxes layin' beside more than a few of the cars, staged an' ready to go. *Each one will have a delivery in it,* he'd said. Thirteen, he'd counted, an' even a couple boxes in the dog cages, too. *Those hold the money,* he'd said.

What had they gotten themselves into, Davis wondered, *an' how in the world were they gonna get outta this mess?*

~*~

Pearly must've rubbed tires against half a dozen auto shops up an' down the highway in Gulfport by lunchtime, but nowhere seemed to be hiring. At least not for a fella his age. All those younger pups had little technical school certifications in new electronic junk, an' unless he wanted to sellout to some lil' pit five-minute oil change work, Mr. Allen didn't feel like his odds to be a good ol' fashioned wrench turner were lookin' too good.

Had he burnt a bridge too soon, he wondered?

154

He'd made good, comfortable money for more than seven or eight years now, an' though the thoughts he'd had recently of makin' it honest without any more of the underhanded stuff was undoubtedly the right one, considerin' Davy, it might not fare out too well for 'em if all the push back got anymore out of hand. Davis had given him Compton's message, and to say he was scared of confrontin' him wasn't necessarily true, but then again he'd heard a recent tale or two about a few meetings that turned into pick-up truck rides, then Back Bay boat rides an' swimmin' trips with gators. What would goin' down there do anyhow? He'd made it clear. He wanted out. He didn't owe 'em anything, money or otherwise. Truth be told, Mr. Allen wasn't sure what all the fuss was about. Sure, he knew 'bout what was goin' on, but he jus' wanted to turn a wrench an' leave them doin' what they saw fit. That could be that. It was simple, wasn't it? Cain't a fella jus' do an honest work, keep his head down an' his nose clean an' let the world turn? Why did him not wantin' to be a part of somethin' make him wrong?

He swung by the gas station an' stepped inside to grab a cold Barq's an' clear his head for spell. It was a good ol' full-service shop, one that still had the old tables an' booths by the window for the old-timers to sip on their coffees first thing every mornin'.

This 'ere, he thought, *is the sorta place I'd have.* Lil' spot for old-timers to sip an' jaw-jack while a few fellas, maybe even Davy, were in the back turnin' wrenches, laughin' 'bout something foolish. 'Course he didn't know nothin' 'bout runnin' no business, what with all the keepin' the books an' all, but if other folks could learn, he could, too.

Before he could think too much more about it, an' started to slide outta the bench, finish his Barq's, an' head back out on the hunt, another fella slid into the bench across from him wearin' a tan polo an' navy blue khakis. Mr. Allen sat up straight an' glanced around before he finally met the eyes of the stranger. His eyes begged the question, but the stranger answered it before it could reach the air.

"Mr. Robert Allen?" he asked. He slid a badge from his pocket onto the table, then slid it back again. "I'm Detective Wes Barnett from the county Sheriff's office. Don't worry, Sir, you ain't in any sort of trouble, yet, but I do have a few questions to ask you."

Mr. Allen sat back in the bench an' tried his best to relax, which came a lot easier than he'd imagined it might. He almost felt relieved...almost.

20

WONDERIN' AN' WANDERIN'

WEDNESDAY MORNING

"Mornin'," Liam said.

Jewel stood like she often did, swaddled in one of Liam's bathrobes, wearin' some god-awful slippers she'd found somewhere, half-chewed by an old stray his momma had let in once years ago. Her hands were wrapped with a death-grip 'round a steamin' cup of coffee, eyes half open. By the bottom of the cup they'd be wide, but right now their golden gleam stayed sheltered away, half-hidden behind the rim of the cup as if the scent itself held some of the caffeine. He set his journal an' bible aside an' took his place leanin' against the porch post so Jewel could sit if she wanted. Half the time she chose to let the door jamb hold her up, the other half she'd take him up on his offer an' rock like she's catchin' up for all those years she never got to.

That was the best thang 'bout bein' a Christian, Liam remembered with a deep breath, soakin' in the smell of the Mississippi pines —every breath of every day is a second chance.

"What's yer plans this morning?" Liam asked.

When she didn't answer right away, he took a sip an' nodded toward the distant woods.

"I's thankin' of headin' over to Fancy's for breakfast, an' then takin' a walk if you'd like."

"Like *in the woods*, in the woods?" she asked. "Or you jus' talkin' in the woods like nex' to 'em?"

"More like *through* 'em. Like we're gonna use 'em to go somewhere."

"You finna use woods like a road?"

"Yep," Liam replied with a laugh.

"You stay doin' some o' the whitest old-man-country-boy sh...*stuff* they is, huh?"

"We can walk on the road if you want, but I figured you'd wanna stay away from the gators, so…"

"Yeah, uh, *no*. You finna show me the wood road, Mr. King. I ain't finna feed 'em no dark meat today," she said with a laugh, strokin' her braids from her face.

"Where you tryna go walkin' through the woods?" she asked. "You tryna sneak me off somewhere? This a date? You tryna play me?" Jewel smirked. *Um-hmm.* "I see dem rosy cheeks an' you hidin' tha smirk behind dat cup, too. Yeah, Mr. King done got caught! He's tryna slide a shirt on a girl."

"How're you so crazy *before* breakfast?"

"Don't be changin' the subject jus' cuz I'm callin' you out! This man said Fancy's an' he know good an' well he be tryna butter me up wit some biscuits."

Liam shook his head. Why his cheeks always betrayed him an' fueled her teasin' he'd never understand. When her eyes settled on him an' he figured she was about done, he finished his cup an' grinned. "Thought we'd head over to the oak side of the river an' visit Travis 'roun' lunchtime. Mr. Montgomery said he'd be that-a-ways with the sitter 'roun' then."

"Oh, so you tryna play both us, huh? I tol' you she fine now you tryna use me ta get her jealous, huh?"

He threw an arm around her an' pulled her into a hug against him as he walked into the kitchen. "What am I gonna do with you, Miss Jewels? Yer 'bout as crazy as they come."

"You forgot one thing, Mr. King," she said as he took their cups an' put them in the sink water. "I'm goin' with Angel an' Tamra today. But hey, I'll still holla at some free breakfast though."

~*~

"Where we at?" Jewels asked, not as excitedly as Liam had hoped, but certainly not as flustered as he'd expected either. These parts of the woods were a lil' rougher than he remembered, an' bein' a city gal he figured she'd 'bout had enough of the rompin' 'round in the woods with the prickly vines an' sticker bushes lickin' at her arms an' legs the whole walk.

"We're only a stone's throw away from the main road," Liam said with a point. Jewel looked at him with a mixture of disbelief.

"I don't even hear no cars," she replied. "You sure somebody ain't gonna come out here shootin' at us?"

"No," he said with a laugh. "This is my land."

"Yours?"

159

"Yeah, I bought this land about two years ago an' I've been makin' payments on a few of the acres I couldn't afford outright. Jus' finally paid 'em off las' month."

"You own this?" she asked, confused. "How much? How far?"

"Ever since we crossed between the barbed wire on that fence back there an' clear to the road," he said. "Ten acres."

"What's an aker?"

"So," he started, scratchin' his head with his cap, "the church?"

Uh-huh...

"That sits on about two acres, parking lot an' all."

"An' you own ten?" she said, an' the way her eyes lit up made him smirk.

"When I's little, me an' my buddy used to come huntin' out here, claimin' all this like it was ours. Built us a tree fort not too far from here. As we grew up, we built a better one in middle school, then we'd live out here all summer. By high school, we had more dreams, bigger dreams, 'bout makin' a business by the roadside like how Marco's is an' all the storefronts. We even thought about openin' a lil' movie theatre."

"Had some parties out here in high school too, huh?"

"Here? Nah. We did all that junk down by the river. This place was secret. Sacred."

"Why you showin' it to me?"

"Jus' wanted to share it with somebody. Don't nobody else really know 'bout it other than Chris an' Angel, an' that's 'cause Angel helped me find the real estate fella. I reckon they forgot all 'bout it by now."

"You gonna clear some out an' build you a house or somethin' one day?"

"I'd like to. But that's expensive an' probably a long time comin'," he replied.

"Yeah, but I bet havin' the land made half of the hard part done, huh?"

"The hard part is finishin' college, first," he laughed.

"Nah, you Superman. You'll do that, too." she said. "The hard part's gonna be findin' some girl ain't tryna use you 'cause you got all the right stuff, an' ten acres."

"You don't think too highly of folks, do ya?" he chuckled.

"An' you too trustin'," Jewels said, shaking her head. "Girls be cuttin'. Lots of girls stay lovin' that bank flow, Mr. King. I'm glad you showed me though, but I'm finna be quick ta tell you don't show it to no girl who don't be lovin' you when she thank you ain't got nothin', first."

~*~

Jewels got more talkative after the first visit to the breakfast buffet.

"An' dis a buffet, too? I ain't never been to a breakfast buffet before. Man, I almos' feel bad playin' you," she teased.

Paige an' her mom were already there before they arrived, an' by the looks of things neither seemed pleased.

"I ain't never seen two white girls wit lattes an' muffins look so sad in my life. Who done died? Some country singer? That Blake boy?"

Liam shook his head. "Blake?"

"Yeah, you know, they stay wit names like Blake or Branch or somethin' woody or stick soundin'. Y'all be lovin' trees an' woods, 'specially 'roun' hur. I'm fer real though. Why she ain't even looked at you twice wit her momma 'round, but her momma lookin' at you like you be owin' her money?"

Now that she'd mentioned it, Paige an' Katy never missed an opportunity to bathe him in at least a smile or two no matter who was nearby. To see her so distraught made him wonder if everything was alright, 'specially with her dad gone travelin' fer business as often as he did. He finished his plate an' waited on Jewel to finish hers before they finally headed toward the door.

"Mornin' Mrs. Jones, Miss Paige," Liam said as they passed. When Paige smirked dimly then looked back to her plate, pickin' at her food with her fork, an' Mrs. Jones' eyes stabbed at him with a scowl, Liam knew Jewel's observations to be as insightful as ever.

"Boy you've got some nerve," she said seethin', like a snake was tryin' to work its way out of her mouth. "Both o' y'all walkin' 'roun' here like the whole town ought ta be proud of ya."

He shouldn't 'ave, but Liam stopped.

"What do you..."

She scoffed. "Don't play dumb, Liam. It don't suit ya. I cain't believe I trusted you 'roun' my daughter all this time."

"Trusted me? Mrs. Jones, I don't know what you've…"

"Save it! You ought ta be ashamed of yerselves."

"Yeah, I bet you think every girl up in here ain't gotta ring on they finger be sleepin' 'roun' too, huh? You rich! Man, bein' kind an' er'body thinkin' he's gettin' wit some girl."

Liam wasn't sure if Mrs. Jones gawked at what Jewel said, her tone, or how loudly she said it. Truth be tol' had Liam not grown used to all three he'd 'ave probably gawked or shied away too.

"You don't deserve him," Paige mumbled.

If Jewel's response shocked Mrs. Jones, Paige's sealed it. "Paige!"

"She don't, Momma! You don't!" she said more boldly, so boldly Liam thought she might stand up. "Before you came things were jus' fine 'round here."

Both hands lifted to her eyes an' she shook her head.

Liam was beside himself. All he could do was gaze at all three of them in turn, speechless.

"*Deserve him?*" Jewels echoed. "Hell, er'body stay knowin' that. Don't nobody in this po-dunk town deserve Liam King, ya heard! See, I tol' you lil' white girls be crazy! Let's go before this thang turns all Jerry Springer up in hur. Lil' mommas start throwin' they lattes an' takin' out earrings." She laughed at her own joke. "Naw, what am I sayin'? It don't get serious roun' hur 'til females be takin' off smart watches."

You don't deserve him...

For a few steps there was silence. He noticed Jewels fidget with her hands an' arms, unsure what she wanted to do with 'em —to shove 'em in her pockets or cross them, but walkin' didn't make either feel right. She glanced to the cracks in the parking lot as they walked down the narrow strip of storefront shops. It hadn't been some dull racist comment, which would've made more sense to a northerner visitin' Mississippi for the first time, or so every movie or TV show made it seem. Liam wondered if a racist comment would've hurt Jewel's feelin's less than flat out bein' tol' she's unworthy of somethin'. What bothered him more was how wrong Paige had been, an' on more than jus' the surface. If only everyone knew what he knew no one would dare say such a thing.

Before they reached Marco's, Angel and Tamra pulled up.

"Perfect timin'," Angel said.

"What *you* doin' today?" Tamra asked.

"Hangin' with my best bud," Liam replied.

"Where is Travis this week with school out? I'm guessin' Mr. Montgomery's at the Park."

"He's with a sitter. I guess they're down by the river. I'm gonna swing by there at lunch."

"Terry an' Chris tol' me what went down," she said a lil' quieter while Jewels walked around an' got in behind Angel. "If you didn't see it comin' you crazy."

"I did. I guess I jus' sort of hoped for somethin' better," he admitted.

"That ain't a bad thing," she said, touchin' his arm. "Stay hopin' like that, lil' bro. We all should stay hopin' like that. Jesus got you! Might not be today, tomorrow, next week, or next month, but He's gonna make it right. Then, folks gonna feel like fools."

His hands dug deep in his jean pockets. "I'll still be covered in mud though."

"Mud washes off better than bein' covered in sin," Tamra replied with a point.

She slid her sunglasses back on her face an' started backin' the car out. "See how I did dat all smooth like that?"

Liam could only shake his head with a smile. Maybe after a day away from it all, he'd be able to focus and know what to do, he hoped. As silly as it sounded, Travis had always been there to give him a new, unexpected perspective on life when everyone around him dug too deep or weighed life like a race an' no matter what happened they'd finish second.

That's what Liam admired so much about his best friend. To Travis winning wasn't about a place or beatin' the next fella, it was about finishing; an' everything inside Liam needed to rediscover that sort of peace an' patience. The faith to finish.

21

SITTIN' IN THE SHADE

WEDNESDAY

"You two ought to be ashamed of yourselves," he heard the words echo in his mind again for the fiftieth time. The scene replayed itself with different responses each time, the next wittier than the last. Some stabbed, others were super-spiritual and filled with scripture to prove a point about gossip, but all-in-all it didn't matter one way or the other. The moment had passed.

Was this what all the mommas and fellas thought about him now? Is this why Pastor Sam had been so calloused 'bout it all an' fired him from every teachin' position? In a way, he'd expected the drama an' the gossip, but he hadn't expected they'd be so openly in his face an' stuck-up about it like they'd caught him with their own two eyes doin' something wrong, or he'd been on the news accused like a school teacher messin' 'round with a student.

Then, to make matters even more dramatic, Paige pulled the whole 'you don't deserve him' mess an' made it sound even more guilty. Not only had she offended Jewels, but

166

made it all emotionally about herself, too, as if Liam had led her to believe something existed between 'em. He tried, unsuccessfully, to take-in a deep, relaxing breath, but before he knew it the familiar path wove back in forth in front of him and the stumps passed underfoot takin' him back to an eternity ago when he'd cut down those trees to make the path alongside his buddies.

He walked a long time in the silence of it all, jus' thinkin' like he did, scroungin' up more ammunition to itch out in his journal later. Liam sighed, shakin' his head as he snapped another stick in hand, rememberin' the trails like yesterday. They seemed so small now, almost like lil' critters had made 'em. He snickered. In a way, they *had* been made by little critters –kids on adventures. A soft trickle tugged him back to the familiar song of the river. He thought about the old church hymn *Peace like a River*, an' how much his momma loved it. More importantly, how much he'd love to have some of that peace right now with everything stirrin' in his mind like a gumbo of gossip.

That's when he could hear the mumblin' of folks talkin' an' a telltale deep laugh echoin' through the woods. There weren't too many who could make Travis laugh like that, he knew. The thought intrigued him. He could count on one hand how many folks Travis even liked to be 'round, much less laugh an' be silly with. Outta all those names, none of 'em where on the other side of the wood line when he stepped from the path onto the sandbar, an' stopped in his tracks. She was a t-shirt with rolled up sleeves, tied up at the arm like when he used to watch her play softball. A long blonde ponytail swayed beneath an' old Harrison ball cap – not a Lady Wildcats cap– a baseball cap, his old cap. Cut-off pants rolled up to the knee danced in ankle-high water, kickin' it back an' forth with Travis at somethin', likely a turtle.

Liam's heart stood still an' tried to beat outta his chest at the same time. Weren't no other ways to explain it, an' he'd probably spend half an hour sittin' in the rockin' chair tryin' to think of a way to write it all out later, but wouldn't find the words, save one. And that word wouldn't capture it enough, not to him. He hadn't seen her in months, an' even then it'd been from afar. She likely hadn't seen or noticed him at all. As he stood there for a split second, he teetered at the thought of slunkin' back into the woods an' hurryin' outta there, but for the life of him he couldn't budge, all he could do was stare at her like he'd never seen her before a day in his life. It was like once his feet touched the sand again, he's trapped there, jus' like the ol' days, watchin' her smilin', hearin' her laugh like it was the best sound in the world. If truth be told there hadn't been a sound he'd ever liked more since the first day he heard her cry. They say without an enemy a person don't really know the value of a friend. The first day he heard her cry they were kids on a playground. After that moment, makin' her laugh had been his daily goal, an' he'd never got tired of tryin'.

All Liam's thoughts about disappearin' back into the woods died when Travis glanced up an' saw him and their worlds collided, joined by the biggest glue God had ever made –Travis.

"Liam!"

He shouted with more joy than a kid on Christmas mornin' and pointed, hoppin' up an' down in the water.

Allie spun, wide-eyed, almost afraid, but she wasn't, was she? Travis clapped with a laugh that echoed off the water, but all Liam an' Allie could do was stare at one another, their mouths gapin' like fishes, searchin' for somethin' to say.

"Hey you," she said, squintin' as she raised a hand to fend the shine from the river.

"Hey you," he said, finally musterin' up the guts.

~*~

They walked from the wood line a couple hours later, Travis between 'em talkin' 'bout the birds an' turtles. Liam couldn't remember the las' time he'd heard Travis talk so much an' stay so happy without so much as a dull moment to rest his mind. Oftentimes, he needed a lil' recharge here an' there, but somethin' 'bout seein' him an' Allie in the same place kept him wound like a kid in a candy store.

Allie had been all smiles at his shenanigans, which came as no surprise. Travis loved to poke an' prod at Liam, tellin' a dozen stories from hittin' the punchin' bag at the Park to the night he tricked Jewels onto the Ferris Wheel.

"You didn't?" Allie said, shakin' her head with a giggle. "I'd a slugged ya good for that one."

"Jewels wasn't too keen on it either, was she, buddy?"

"Nope. Liam said he's gonna get 'er fer messin' with his buddy, an' he did! You did, huh, Liam!"

"Sure did! Don't nobody mess with my buddy!"

"An' we saw Ms. Jewels the other day, too, huh Allie-girl?"

"Yep, she came with grandad, didn't she?"

"Yep!" Travis said. "I like her. Her skin's shiny an' pretty like a, like a, like a...."

He held his forefinger in a circle with his thumb, strugglin' to find the word.

"Like a marble," Liam finished.

"Yeah! Like a marble. Shiny an' pretty."

"She's silly an' funny, too, huh?"

169

"Yeah. She talks funny, too."

"Where's she from?" Allie asked.

"Indianapolis,"

"No family or nothin' huh?"

"None she knows of, or she's mentioned. None close like what we know."

"She's had it pretty rough, huh?"

"Yeah, I think that's why she's not too quick to wanna head back up that way. It's not too often folks get a chance at a fresh start."

"It's a lot easier when there's nothin' holdin' 'em back," Allie said. She glanced away an' at the high grass an' Liam couldn't help but wonder what she meant. Did she mean her an' Kelli? Or Him? Or...nothin' at all? *She's probably jus' talkin' 'bout Jewels, ya eijet!*

"D'ya ever thank 'bout leavin' once yer folks moved off to Haiti?"

"A few times, but nothin' ever stuck."

"Why not? 'Fraid you might miss it all?"

"Things. Yeah."

"People?"

There was somethin' there in the question —an opportunity, an' Liam felt it— but as soon as it jostled his heart a lil' his tongue jumbled it up.

"I dunno. The idea of startin' over somewhere new, surrounded by all new faces an' places jus' seems overwhelmin' to me," Liam said. "I'd rather share somethin' like that with someone. What about you?"

Her ponytail waved back an' forth. "I couldn't leave momma, or this house, even. It's all we know. There's something comfortable in that, don't ya think?"

"Yeah," he said with a nod.

"Yep!" Travis agreed. "Couches is comfortable, too."

"You ready for a nap or somethin', Mister?" Allie said with a laugh.

"Lunch an' Crawtaters," he said with an' uplifted finger. "Then, a nap."

"Man's got a plan, *Allie-girl!*" Liam said liftin' his finger like Travis.

"Yeah, *Allie-girl!*" Travis echoed.

The back door still squeaked.

"'Bout time! I's 'bout to send out the...well, lookie there!" Ms. Luanne said with a holler then a cackle-of-a-laugh.

"Found a stray," Allie said.

"Las' time you brought home a stray it had fleas,"

"I'm pretty sure this one has all his shots," Allie replied. "Tea?"

"Might have a few fleas, too," Liam said with a smile. He nodded with a 'definitely' sort of expression on his face, as if passin' up the chance would be the biggest mistake he'd ever make. Ms. Luanne buried herself in Liam's frame an' gave him a hug only a momma could give. It said so many things. It asked him why he'd ever stopped comin' by; it apologized for anything she'd ever said to make him feel like he hadn't been welcome, an' it begged him to stay.

"Well, I suppose we can keep him then," she said. Ms. Luanne turned so quick he couldn't make it out for sure, but Liam thought he saw a tear or two linger there.

"I'm sleepin' on the couch!" Travis said, matter-of-factly. "You're sleepin' with Allie-girl!" He laughed like the thought seemed yucky, which it likely did to Travis.

The kitchen stopped an' Liam was pretty sure they could've heard a pin drop. Allie sort of choked on her tea, hidin' her face behind it while a rosy tint spread to her cheeks.

He pretended not to notice.

"Nuh-uh!" he replied, pretendin' to be jus' as grossed out as Travis. "She prob'ly snores louder than a freight train. An' steals the sheets, too! I'll sleep on the porch swing."

"Outside? With the critters?"

"I bet she snores so loud even the critters might run," Liam said.

"A good pop in the nose might make *you* snore tonight, you keep talkin'," Allie said.

"Yes ma'am," Liam replied. He looked at Travis with wide eyes.

"He's 'fraid! Liam's 'fraid of Allie-girl…"

"Always 'ave been," Liam mumbled. Allie hid her face behind her cup again.

Ms. Luanne chuckled at the sink.

22

RIVER LAIR SNARE

WEDNESDAY NIGHT

M usic echoed across the river, louder than the sound of the water flowin' by, but not so loud the distant neighbors might hear or call about it. Not that they thought anybody might actually come with Spring Break still goin' on keepin' all the police down by the traffic and the crowds. Reports of shootin's, lootin', an' theft were everywhere up an' down the coast, but most of that stayed buried from the headlines. The shootin's didn't, but the burglaries or the way things were trashed always did. Bad publicity. Stuff they'd write papers on in a few weeks in English class, but no one thought about now.

Dillon pumped two Dixie cups from the keg, handed one to Paige and lifted his toward Davis. He'd laughed lots, tryin' to shake off what he'd heard an' learned that mornin', Davis knew, but the twinge of fear in his eyes tol' Davis they were far from done talkin' 'bout it all. After all, a party was a party...there'd be time for all that muck later when the girls in tight jeans weren't around.

And though his brain tol' him different, an' the thoughts of his ol' man kept him distracted more than he'd like to admit, Davis couldn't deny the sight of bein' persuaded by Kat an' the swayin' she did in the sand to the rhythm of the music. There'd be plenty of time to worry 'bout his ol' man tomorrow.

Kat curled a finger for him to come dance with her. Like a bass on a line, he'd been hooked, but unlike every bass he'd ever known, he didn't put up a fight. Didn't want to. Not with *that* look in her eyes. They kissed and danced along with everyone else for a few songs 'til some eejit put on a ridiculous song an' ruined the mood. The whole crowd growled a complaint.

"Want another one?" Davis asked. He kissed Kat an' took her cup from her hand while she nodded, still eyein' him like she had before.

"Don't be too long," she said.

He met Dillon at the kegs.

"Where's Paige?" Davis asked.

"Had to walk away an' answer her phone. Her folks were callin'. Cora Lynn went with her." He added the last part because he knew that'd be Davis's next question. Neither Kat nor Paige knew the heads or tails of the woods or how to get anywhere. They'd both said they were gonna be at Cora Lynn's tonight, but both boys knew they wouldn't even see her house, much less sleep in it.

They filled the Dixie cups and lifted 'em to one another. Davis ignored the glance Dillon gave him, remindin' him they still had stuff to talk about. But all those thoughts, even the alluring eyes of Kat, rushed out of his head when he turned and gazed into the big blue eyes of beauty. He almost gasped. Allie stood with her arms crossed, an' a look on her face that tiptoed dangerously close to a parent, the responsible kind, the ones Davis had seen in movies.

He even felt nervous holdin' the cups.

Uhhh! The sound crept out while words choked their way between his lips. She had that expression again, the same one she'd had when she handed him the bag of cans an' tol' him he was better than all that. Why she thought 'bein' better' had anything to do with puttin' a few beers back, he didn't rightly understand, but it'd only take a quick breath or two for Kat to spot a ponytail standin' between her an' him an' she'd be there, he knew.

"Hey!" he managed to say, finally. "How are you? How's Ms. Luanne?"

"Yeah, uh, good," Allie replied, noddin'. "What're ya doin' here Davy?"

"Jus'," he waved a hand around toward his other teammates as if the gesture alone might explain itself so he didn't have to. "You know, hangin' with friends."

"Friends, huh?"

"Yeah," he caught sight of her cap, "we're on the baseball team together. Season starts next week. We've got a scrimmage game on Friday. You should come."

If Allie showed any interest in chattin' 'bout baseball, Davis didn't notice. By the look on her face you'd think she hated the sport or anything like it.

"Hey, I'm real sorry 'bout the other day," he said. "We didn't know those guys were gonna..." He stopped explainin' when she shook her head dismissively.

"Ain't none of my business," she said. "'S jus' doin' what my momma wanted me to. She can't suffer any of that junk any more than we can suffer spiders or snakes to live. Jus' assume stomp an' shoot every livin' one. We do appreciate all y'all did though," she said. "Truly."

"So, if you ain't drinkin' or partyin', why'd you come?"

She never had a chance to answer. Kat circled Allie an' took her spot beside Davis, slidin' the drink from his hand. She put her arm around him, claimin' her territory.

"A few of the girls are goin' down the river with the guys. Wanna come?" Kat whispered to him, ignoring Allie.

It was a test, Davis knew. Girls always did this sort of thing to flex. If the boy didn't ignore the other girl, they'd wish they had before the night was over. Every demon in hell couldn't hold back the rage of a girl bein' treated like a second to another, hotter girl like Allie. And, unfortunately, how he reacted now could either add a ridiculous amount of drama to his already dramatic life or help ease it in more than a few creative ways. Seein' as how his chances with Allie seemed about as distant and likely as walkin' to the other side of the river on top of the water, Davis chose the easier of the two options. He smiled at Kat and nodded at Allie.

"Well, it was good seein' ya," he said. Then, Davis jus' sort of turned and walked away with Kat down the sand. He didn't even look back.

Cora Lynn was there a second later, followin' Allie's eyes back and forth from Davis to Paige and Dillon, an' what appeared to be the closest thing Mississippi had to seein' a volcanic eruption. She tucked a few strands of loose hair behind her ears and crossed her arms nervously like Allie, then shuffled her feet in the sand.

"Her momma jus' called," Cora Lynn clarified. "Said she'd called my momma an' found out she hadn't seen us all night."

"So, it's started then, huh?" Allie replied, with a sigh.

Cora Lynn nodded an' Allie didn't miss the sadness in her expression.

"You're doin' the right thing, girl. Don't think for a secon' these girls ain't gonna have to live with the mistakes they could make out here, 'cause there ain't a woman alive doesn't wish somewhere in the back of her mind she'd had at least one good friend like you at some point who would've stopped her from climbin' in a truck with some stupid drunk boy back in high school."

"Yeah, I know it was my idea an' all, but I still cain't help but feel like a snitch," Cora Lynn admitted.

"Yeah," Allie replied with a contorted expression that showed how stupid she thought all that 'snitchin' nonsense was, "but to adults you look like a seat belt."

"They say snitches get stitches," Cora Lynn said with a wince.

"I've had stitches...an' I'll take them over a stretcher any day."

"What're you doin' out here?" Cora Lynn asked, suddenly realizing this hadn't been part of their plan.

Allie shrugged. "Figured you might want someone to talk with back to the house so your momma could see you spendin' time with a friend."

"Tryin' to cover my tracks, huh? Weren't gonna leave me for dead like the other night?" she laughed.

"Somethin' like that," Allie said, flashin' a smirk.

Cora Lynn's expression at the thoughtfulness of it all brightened Allie's mood, but then suddenly took an unexpected turn.

"I think I'm gonna wait here with 'em," she said.

Allie looked like she'd been smacked.

Huh? "Why won't you jus' let 'em get caught? Why'd you have to be here, too?" Allie asked, confused. "Now you're gonna get punished right alongside 'em, and you're the one tryin' to make things right."

Cora Lynn shrugged. "Guess I just figured I'm guilty of all them other times jus' the same. Not gettin' caught back then don't mean I wasn't wrong with 'em. Hopefully, them bein' caught now will give me the chance to show 'em what I already learned. Besides, if they's caught an' I wasn't, they likely wouldn't listen to me otherwise."

Allie didn't have anything to say. All she could do was stare at Cora Lynn dumbfounded. Part of her wanted to smack some sense into the girl, but there was another part there, too. A more familiar one. She saw his face then, the distraught hopeless expression of a kid who'd tried an' failed miserably. It was like lookin' at the leftovers of a popped balloon wonderin' if it might put itself back together an' fill up, again. Only Allie knew somethin' like that would be nonsense. Didn't even sound right! As her memories of Liam's tired, swollen red eyes looked up from the steps of the church all those years ago, she could feel the holes in him like stickin' her fingers through a ripped shirt. He'd jus' wanted to be guilty alongside 'em —to be the friend who'd done it all from start to finish, even the punishment.

Not because he'd liked to be punished, but because, like Cora Lynn, he felt he'd deserved it.

And in some weird way, as Allie thought about everyone who'd been there on that day, judgin' an' bein' judged, he'd been the only one who thought like Jesus. In all her Sunday school lessons, an' all the preachin' she'd heard up to that point, Liam had been the only one willin' to sacrifice it all for his friends, even if it meant makin' himself like them when they needed it most. He'd been the one fightin' against them doin' the wrong things the entire time, the one who'd secretly loved her more than Kenny ever had. He coulda sat back an' shook his head with that 'I told ya so' look on his face, an' been right. But even after that day, he continued to stick his neck out again an' again to keep 'em all together because he knew somethin' they didn't –they needed one another more than ever.

But jus' like with Jesus, nobody really listened. Sure, they read the bible an' thought awful highly of it, but nobody really liked doin' it like Jesus did. Livin' like he did. Lovin' like he did.

Then, Kenny died.

And after all these years Liam still cared like it'd all happened yesterday.

As the tears began to trickle from her eyes, Cora Lynn's expression changed from sad to confused, and then mortified.

"I-I'm sorry, Allie…"

Allie lifted her hand, swiped her cheek, an' mustered a smile.

"No honey! It ain't…I ain't all," she waved a hand at her mess-of-a-face. "This ain't 'cause of you," she tried to explain. "You didn't do a thing wrong, girl," she said wrappin' her in a hug. "Not a thing. I'm so proud of you for stickin' by yer friends when they need you the most. Keep stickin'."

Allie held Liam then as she held Cora Lynn, and she prayed to God he'd give her the chance to hold Liam that way one day, too.

~*~

"So, what did Allie Quaves want?" Kat asked once they were down the river a lil' ways.

"I dunno. I don't rightly know how she even knew we's havin' somethin' down here?"

179

Kat's expression showed she wasn't convinced by his answer, but Davis jus' shrugged, an' took another sip from his cup.

"Me an' my ol' man been workin' on her house all week."

"*Her* house? That's the house where yer truck flipped?"

"Yeah,"

Kat laughed. "She lives in that dump?"

Right then Davis almost said somethin' he would have regretted, maybe, but held his tongue. He'd been in that house, seen the memories an' the history there. His ol' man had shown him 'bout Catfish an' the life him an' Ms. Luanne had given Allie. '*That dump*' echoed in his ears for more steps than he could count.

But that was how girls could be when they felt threatened by prettier girls, Davis knew. Those pretty lil' manicured nails turned into knives quicker than a dog might snap if ya touch its ears.

After a minute Paige came down the beach in tears an' Davis could feel the drama followin' like a wave of heat from a bonfire. He took his cue, an' Kat's cup, then headed back down toward the kegs for another round. Before he made it Dillon met him.

"Dude, we've got a serious problem," he said.

"I tol' you two kegs wouldn't be enough for the whole team."

"Not that," Dillon said with a wave of his hand. "Paige an' Kat's families...they know."

23

BURIED EMBERS

THURSDAY MORNING

Davis grumbled, stretchin' his arms under his pillow before he rolled over an' rubbed the sleep from his eyes. He'd heard Pearly start up in the back of his mind, in that mid-dream world where he didn't quite care enough to wake up. Like some sort of cue, his phone buzzed to life less than a minute later.

"Well, las' night was stupid!" Dillon said.

"Mornin' sunshine,"

"Shut yer face. I'm serious. All 'em parents showed up. We're done now! Ain't no way nobody's ever comin' to one of our parties again."

"So what. I'd rather jus' chill at the house or on the sand with a couple folks than the whole team anyhow," Davis said.

"Come on, man! I'm serious!"

"Me, too," he replied. "Us an' a six-pack is how this whole thang started anyhow."

"An' what about the girls?"

"What about 'em?"

"They're parents will skin 'em alive. Mine's already gonna take the truck an' maybe even the phone."

Davis could only sigh at the whinin'. His ol' man would care an' all, but things had been too crazy to keep track of all the other parent junk. Besides, who's mad at who an' parents all callin' one another...if anybody had his dad's number he'd be shocked. He hadn't even been on the team call list whenever the coach rescheduled practices or games.

"My phone's been blowin' up all mornin'. Some of the guy's folks even called coach, man. This is big."

"So what? D'ya think this means we won't play or somethin'?" Davis sort of laughed. "The whole team was there Dill-weed. We get benched, who's playin'?"

"Might could shut down the program."

"An' lose booster money an' the coach not get paid? Come on, use yer head for somethin' other than sittin' yer hat on. They're not gonna take away a whole program 'cause some kids had a party that nobody got hurt at."

"That's easy fer you to say! Yer ol' man..."

"Hey! You're actin' like a sissy! Man up. Don't get yer panties all bunched up, Mary. You sound like Kat an' Paige. This ain't life-or-death."

Dillon took a second, jostlin' the phone around while he was doin' somethin', then after a minute his tone sounded a lil' more relaxed.

"Look man," Davis said. "Does it suck? Sure. But this ain't gonna be nothin' a week or so from now. Hell, I bet by Monday mornin' when school starts back an' practice begins, this'll be like a fart in the wind."

Dillon snickered. "*Fart in the wind?* Where'd you come up with this stupid crap?"

Davis laughed. "Jus' pulled it out my butt, I reckon."

"That's 'bout where yer brains are anyhow?"

"You're one to talk! Your head's been shoved up yours for a while now."

"Says the fella who cain't take a curve without dumpin' his truck through a fence."

"Yeah, yeah, yeah. I'll holler at ya later. Gotta get ready for my big day."

"Why? Whatcha got goin' on today?"

"Got a date."

"A date? With who?"

"Yer mom."

"Shut yer face!"

Davis hung up with a laugh an' tossed his sheets aside. Truth was he didn't know what might happen with the team, or if the school would even care too much. He'd only heard rumors about how prom parties and other home bashes went south an' folks got punished, but never nothin' like this. Kat would be a wreck. Paige, too. That'd make things stupid for a while, but the longer he thought about it with the hot water beatin' on his back in the shower, the more an' more he didn't really care. They were fun, but nothin' all lovey-dovey. Nothin' like what they make it seem like in movies or what love sounds like when he'd heard old folks talk about it —all butterflies an' smiles.

All he kept seein' was the deep dark stare of Allie glarin' at him. He'd pretended not to care at the time, on the account of keepin' Kat where he wanted her 'til the night ended, but even that didn't end the way it had a few times before.

Now, he wasn't so sure.

Allie had never been there before that night. He would've remembered her. Every guy there would've remembered her. But why *had* she been there? The thought ate at Davis more an' more 'til all he could make heads or tails of was the way she'd hid the bag of cans. Why'd she care so much? Maybe she did like him, only didn't know how to say? Nah. Girl like her wouldn't be shy, an' surely wouldn't be shy 'round a high school boy. It was something else. Somethin' Davis couldn't put his finger on. Another one of 'em past stories that still didn't quite add up.

~*~

Young an' old, the mechanics paused an' watched, washin' their hands with dark greasy rags, while Bob Allen strode through the shop like a man on a mission. He had a rolled-up slip of paper in his hand, an' nodded at only a few of the men, the ones he knew weren't partial or ridin' the fence. Compton hadn't called him, an' unless a fella or two had been followin' him —which he hadn't ruled out entirely— the boss likely didn't have a clue he was coming. Regardless, he didn't seem the least bit surprised when Bob stopped at the door jamb an' leaned on it nonchalantly with a knock, jus' like ol' times. Like nothin' had changed.

"Well, I'll be…" Compton said. He slid his readin' glasses off his face an' rocked back in the old metal office chair. It relented beneath his weight with a squeak of some big spring.

"Whatcha say, Bob?"

"Gotta tow truck hitchin' up my boy's truck, gonna haul it over to Eugene's in Gulfport. Gave me a lil' better price. Said they might could have it done over the weekend. This'll put that knucklehead back out on the road an' back an' forth to ball practice sooner, which means outta my hair. Cain't have him stealin' Pearly all week."

"Well, that's a bit of a slap in the face, don't ya say? Won't even bring it to yer own shop?"

"Nah. Y'all are a might busier than Eugene's, an' what with all the nonsense with Cheesy an' Buckwheat, an' what you tol' my boy an' his pal the other day, I'd say it's fair to keep things a bit more civil. Don't want nobody getting' all cowardly an' takin' a stab at me through my boy."

"Civil?"

"Yeah. If we got issues don't mean he does."

"I'd say it does, Bob. Like it or not, your problems might bubble over an' splatter on him. Bein' close to the pot might still getcha burnt."

Mr. Allen chuckled. "Well, I suppose this is where I could say 'put a lid on it' then, an' not be wrong. 'Cause if you think threatenin' my boy or his truck is gonna fly, you ain't as bright as the dim bulb I had you out for in the first place."

"Careful, Bob. Where'd all that civil talk head off to?"

"Still civil. Jus' settin' the rules. Y'all gotta problem with me wantin' to keep my head down an' work an honest man's job, that's one thing. Draggin' my boy in is another. Y'all touch my boy, I'll put every las' one of ya in a box."

"That's hefty talk," he said with a smirk-of-a-challenge.

"Jus' settin' the rules. I said 'out', I meant it. I don't owe anyone anything, an' you know that."

"Cain't jus' walk away, Bob. You know too much, an' that gets some of these lil' fellas all twitchy."

"I don't care. Let 'em be twitchy. Shouldn't be hirin' no druggies anyhow. Got a dad-gummed shop to run."

"You know jus' as well as I do havin' a few druggies to run stuff keeps things easier, an' lil' cuts here an' there keeps 'em loyal. Besides, the good ol' mechanics are still 'round to get the real work done."

"Cain't jus' let me be one of the good ol' mechanics?" He chuckled. "It's like havin' a player who can play two positions great pick one when you need the other, an' the next best guy isn't even half as good. I've only got a couple really good, reliable fellas, and I've got a few more great mechanics. Only a few. If you step over into the mechanic side only, I'm up the creek on a reliable fella to keep the shipments goin'."

"I see where that puts ya, Compton, I really do. But I made it clear an' I meant it. Choose one of these other knuckleheads who don't care 'bout their family all that much, an' let 'em be yer next fella. I ain't that guy anymore."

The tow truck pulled around the building with the Goblin on it. Bob Allen took a couple steps into the room and dropped the paper on the desk with a 'we're finished' nod.

"You're makin' a mistake," Compton said lowly. "Cheesy an' Buckwheat tol' you what I said. Nobody gets out."

"I am," Bob Allen replied. "An' this is the las' day you'll see my face here."

"Las' day a lot of folks might see yer face, if you're gettin' me."

"It is what it is," he replied.

Pearly eased up behind the tow truck an' Bob Allen waved at the driver to head out. He'd follow him down, past Marco's an' the main street, through the four-way, past the church, an' down an' around the bar he used to frequent on the riverside, then clear on to Eugene's in Gulfport only lookin' in the rear view mirror a couple times. The tape was itchy under his shirt, snaggin' at a few too many hairs. He'd never see the dozen or so unmarked cars peel into the shop, or the Sheriff's deputies with Detective Barnett.

The ones who tried to make a run for it out the back door ran into the officers already positioned on the dirt road, some parked in the exact same spot Dillon and Davis had the day before, waitin', listenin' to the wiretap as Compton stacked the evidence against himself. Every detail from the toolboxes to where they kept the money an' the shipments in the oil change pits were raided for the better part of the day. More than two dozen arrests were made, an' by the end of the day the largest dealers on the Mississippi Gulf Coast were behind bars, an' though Bob Allen would still have to appear in county court to plea his own case, havin' been in the mix of it all, he'd at least be able to sleep at home 'til that day came.

Compton had been right. It was the las' day a lot of folks in that shop saw his face.

24

SIDELINES

THURSDAY MORNING

Liam sat up in a cold sweat and swiped the sheets off him with a sigh. He was there again, at the river when he stood up to Kenny for the first time. Before that he'd never had the nerve, never thought he could or should. But everything had been fallin apart around him an' all Liam thought he could do was stand there and watch while Kenny's ol' man drank himself stupid an' the death of his momma still tore at him. They'd tried to keep him busy an' laughin' as much as they could, but time was jus' tickin' away an' he didn't seem to be snappin' outta the cycle of things. Kenny was like a brother to him, and brothers were supposed to be more than spectators. Standin' on the sidelines had never been Liam or Kenny's strength, not when they could get in the game an' play.

If only he'd told someone. If only he'd said more or done more maybe Kenny would still be there today?

A noise downstairs stirred him from his thoughts.

Jewels sat on the couch, facin' away from the stairs, her bag in her hands. She'd taken everything out of it and laid it on the coffee table. A wallet with her driver's license, a few shoppin' cards she'd had before she left Indy, nothin' big, a debit card. Liam hadn't paid too much attention to 'em. He felt odd standin' there watchin' her, like he's snoopin' or something, so he eased back up the stairs an' then made a louder noise and crashed his feet down as he walked. Jewels didn't change anything, not that he'd thought she might hide something or anything. Her golden eyes met his.

"You ain't sleepin' good?" she asked.

He shook his head. "Had a dream. You?"

She motioned a hand toward the things on the table. "When I's out with Tamra an' Angel yesterday I jus' realized I don't want none of dis anymore, but I don't know what I should keep."

"We might be able to get you a new driver's license an', if you want, we could look for a job?"

"I had a couple jobs at fast food places, but I only worked a week or two. They's..." she stopped herself and took in a breath, changin' her mind. "*I* didn't do things right. I didn't go on time or work very hard. I jus' sort of complained the whole time 'cause they wouldn't let me on my phone."

"Ain't jus' you, Jewels. All those temps we have at the Fun Park are the same way."

"I know, but then I see you workin' hard, knowin' people, an' I think people be ignorin' there's other ways to live. In Indy we ain't like dat... like dis." She waved a hand around. "Liam, dis house so pretty. Dis town so small an' the people be different. All my friends would call it crusty or boring, but it be nice not havin' to watch my back or knowin' I can trus' you an' Tamra an' Angel —even though she fried."

189

They shared the laugh, but Jewels only turned toward him and pulled her legs crisscross on the couch. "I-I jus' wanna new life. I feel like I's given somethin' new here an' like I'm in a movie wit you. You know?"

Liam nodded. "Yeah, but I gotta tell you truth, Jewels. Jus' like in those movies there's a lot of things missin' you don't know, yet. Things I ain't had the chance to tell you."

"Like what?"

"Like things about me. 'bout my past."

"You think I wanna tell *you* every-thang 'bout who I was?" she replied with a lifted brow.

"No."

"Right! See? You don't owe me anything, Liam. Jus' like I learned Sunday. You ain't who you been. They see you wrong an' *they* doin' *you* wrong. That ain't you. Tha' lil' white girl was wrong, but she be right too. I don't deserve you, but the way you acted was like you's some piece of trash an' you ain't worthy of anything. She's wrong fer sayin' I'm trash an' don't deserve you —an' she lucky I didn't make her swallow her teeth— but you's jus' as wrong for believin' the other side, too. You ain't trash, bruh! See, I meant what I said. Dis town don't deserve you. You really is a king, an' tha' girl you love, Allie, you need to let her be your queen. Whatever you did tha' you think is so bad, she done forgave you."

Liam shook his head. "I don't think she..."

"Boys be stupid for real! Look, she *really* likes you. It's like she's been sittin' in tha' old house like she a Disney princess waitin' on you to come rescue her. Get yo head out yo..." she waved her hand to keep herself from cursin'.

How many years had they missed jus' waitin', Liam wondered? They used to be so close. Did they even know each other anymore? What if they'd changed? He thought about the mornin' with Travis an' the laughs, how odd it all felt to see her an' know the time had passed, but also feel as if it'd been only yesterday since they'd walked next to the river as teenagers.

"You saw somebody dump me outta car, an' didn't think but a hot minute to take off ya shirt an' cover me, an' carry me to yo crib...but now you's actin' like dis is tough? You be walkin' between me an' gators, but you tellin' ol' girl you love her *is hard?*"

She tilted her head like he'd said something stupid, but as usual, Liam hadn't been allowed to say a word.

"I'm 'bouts ta start my whole life over up in hurr an' you is Superman! Y'all know you need ta start yo life wit me 'round, an' keep me company. Girl tryna see her first Mississippi weddin'! I bet y'all fried! Wearin' flannel an' camo dresses an' ponytails an' baseball hats."

Liam couldn't help but laugh.

"They be servin' biscuits at the reception, too. Watch! I'm finna ask Monte to be my date, too."

She smiled seein' Liam smile, and it felt good to talk to someone about it all, someone who knew better than most what it meant to start over an' to be afraid. So many had chosen to turn their backs on the character of people, Liam realized, but not jus' that, the grace an' mercy of a life dedicated to bein' a Christian.

"You really are a Jewel you know?" Liam said. He walked over to her and gave her a hug, buryin' her head in his chest.

~*~

Liam walked to the Fun Park by mid-morning, opened the office an' garages, and began the daily tinkerin' on the karts, before Mr. Montgomery rolled in an hour later.

"What you doin' 'ere so early? Got somewhere to be later?"

"Nah, jus' figured I'd get an early stab at it. How's my buddy this mornin'?"

Mr. Montgomery smiled from ear to ear. "Wouldn't stop yappin' 'bout how much fun he had yesterday, what with you showin' up down by the river an' all."

'Yeah, 'bout that," Liam said. "I tol' you I's headin' down that-a-way to see him…"

Uh-huh?

"Why didn't you tell me who Travis' sitter was?"

"Why? Would that've mattered?"

"I… maybe…" Liam struggled to find the words, jumbled aroun' between his head an' his heart.

Pfff! Mr. Montgomery sounded with a dismissive wave. "Quit bein' a sissy 'bout it. Y'all gotta face tha' mess someday anyhow. I reckon it's been 'bout long enough, what'ya say? Quit wadin' through all that ol' mess an' let the water under the bridge where it belongs, son. Ain't a secret you love the gal, always have! An' she has feelin's for you too, though I'm sure yer too dad-gummed stubborn ta see 'em. Reckon Travis would see 'em 'fore you did."

"It ain't that easy,"

"Boy, if you weren't as big as a grizzly, I'd slap the stupid outta you. An' I got half-a-mind ta do it anyhow. Take me all dad-gummed day, but you'd feel a load better once all that stupid done ran off."

"I was Kenny's best friend. She was Kenny's girl…"

"An' the whole world knew he was headed in a spiral she wasn't gonna follow. Y'all tried for weeks to pull him out, but you cain't fix what don't wanna be fixed, bud. Not to mention the fact you loved her more from the get-go."

"That's what made it hard…"

"You gonna pretend like I ain't been 'ere the whole time an' tell me some sob story?"

"No Sir, I jus'..."

"I's there when Bob Allen's wife passed an' their whole family went haywire; when they found out 'bout Allie-girl an' Kenny a year later; I's there the night of the wreck; I's there the day of the funeral, an' I's even millin' 'round with some other church fellas tryin' ta get ol' Bob Allen back in his right mind, too. An' none of that's sayin' nothin' 'bout all the visits I's makin' to Ms. Luanne an' Allie-girl checkin' up on 'em when everybody else tossed 'em out like warm coleslaw."

Liam hung his head an' listened.

"Now, look 'ere," Mr. Montgomery said, cockin' his head to draw Liam's eyes back to his. "I know what you did, but I also know what you did for that girl when nobody else would. When Ms. Luanne was sick, how you went with Allie to the doctor's appointments, an' even to the hospital the night sweet lil' Kelli came to us. Ms. Luanne couldn't, others wouldn't, but you did. You's jus' a boy back then, Liam, but I'd be a fool if I said you weren't actin' like more of a man than most I know."

"But then my folks found out, an' the..."

"I know. Jus' like what you're dealin' with now with Jewel an' all the hogwash, but Jesus dealt with churchy knuckleheads like them back in the day, too –pharisees more concerned with how they appeared than where their hearts were."

"D'ya think I's wrong to..."

"Nope," Mr. Montgomery interrupted. "Son, for a young man still in school an' under the authority of his folks, livin' under *their* roof, you've gotta honor that authority. They said stop goin' round, you stopped. Scripture says that was the right thing to do, even if their reasons might not've been. Everything inside you wanted to be there more an' more for her, for *them*, but you were put between a rock an' a hard place, an' unfortunately the choices were made for ya."

He put his hand on Liam's shoulder an' gave it a hard squeeze.

"You haven't done wrong by anyone," he said. "But I'd be lyin' if I said you weren't tryin' harder than anyone to dig yerself outta some hole you ain't even in. For the life of me, son, I ain't never seen a fella so buried in undeserved guilt. Who d'ya feel like you owe somethin' to?"

Liam choked at the words, shakin' his head. Tears started to sneak up, an' he cleared his throat more than once tryin' to shove 'em back.

"I gave Kenny the keys that night," he said, ashamed. "I let Allie in the truck. We almos' hit Travis on the road. Someone died 'cause of *me*. We *all* coulda died 'cause of me."

Mr. Montgomery sat silently for a second, takin' in a deep breath. For a while the honks and music bumpin' up an' down Beach Blvd had faded to the background, but now grew to an overwhelming crescendo, once again.

"You didn't raise Kenny to drink. You didn't cause his momma to pass, or his old man to lose hope an' forget he needed to be there for his son. You didn't put those beers in Kenny's hands that night an' then talk him into drivin'. You didn't make him start the truck, or make Allie make the bad choice to get in it. You didn't forget an' leave the front door unlocked so Travis could sneak out to find his sailboat he left at the river in the middle of the night. You got in the truck with your best friend when he was hurtin', confused, an' needed a friend, even though you knew how reckless an' stupid it was."

"That was really stupid."

"Ya think?"

Liam snickered, swipin' a few tears away.

"You know, Jewel said jus' 'bout the same thing you did this mornin'. Not with all the details an' whatnot, but about Allie, an' lettin' the past be the past an' the future be the future."

"She'd know better than most right now, I reckon. She's a sharp gal," he replied. "With your visit yesterday, I heard how excited Travis was, an' I could tell by the expression on Allie's face while he was carryin' on before we could get to the truck she had a fun time, too. What about you?"

"It was like nothin' had changed. Like we're kids again, skippin' rocks by the water, laughin' an' jokin' 'bout nothin' an' everything."

"Lovebirds, huh?"

Liam smiled, not sure how to respond.

"Well, aight then, Lovebird. Let's quit all this chirpin' an' get all this setup before we open shop. Thursdays are the Fridays before Fridays. Come a few hours this place ought to look like a wasp's nest."

25

A BREAK IN THE CLOUDS

THURSDAY AFTERNOON

Davis imagined himself walkin' clear out to Ms. Luanne's jus' to talk with Allie; to ask more questions an' maybe get to the bottom of what all this jumbled mess in the back of his mind was tryin' to sort out. He'd planned on jus' snatchin' Pearly for an' hour or so, but wherever the ol' man was, he sure wasn't answerin' his phone. So, he flipped through some channels, started his laundry, raided the fridge at lunchtime, an' even wandered 'round the yard a bit before he finally settled back in the trailer an' plopped down on the couch, again.

His life hadn't been so boring before he got a phone an' a truck, had it?

When he couldn't shake the thoughts of the girls –Kat an' Paige an' Allie– all dancin' 'round in his head, he started to wonder 'bout his ol' man an' how crazy things had been with him lately, then a whole other bomb exploded. *Is that*

why the ol' man wasn't pickin' up his phone? Had somethin'
happened? Had he gone to see Compton after all?

Dillon would be grounded from his truck, like he'd said.
There wasn't anyone else he could think of who'd be able to
give him a ride. He might could ride his bike, but that'd jus'
be downright embarassin', like one of 'em old men who
couldn't drive 'cause they got a DUI so they rode those
scooter things instead. It'd be like ridin' the school bus as a
senior, an' Davis had a lil' more self-dignity than to stoop
down that low.

The longer he thought about it, the more stirred up he
got to get answers, but the less motivation he found to *do*
anything. Instead, Davis jus' huffed out a sigh of frustration
on the couch, rocked his head back an' stared at the *click,*
click, click of the ceilin' fan whirrin' 'round for what felt like
an eternity 'til his eyes fell back to the partial glimpse of his
ol' man's bed beyond the propped open door. Hadn't been
but a few nights earlier he'd seen the old cedar chest for the
second time lyin' open, an' that'd been jus' as odd as
everything else —the work at the house; the rummagin'
through the garage, an' even the memories of the trucks an'
his momma.

Before he knew where his legs were takin' him, Davis
was up an' in the room, then on his knees an' slidin' the chest
out from beneath the bed across the old shaggy carpet. He
flipped the lid back an' took in that smell all over again, the
one that'd reminded him of his momma. He couldn't
remember her all that much anymore, an' even those
memories might not be actual ones, jus' bits an' pieces of
stories or somethin' from pictures he'd imagined in his mind.
Some other time that might bother him, but truth be tol'
he'd jus' assume have somethin' rather than nothin'.

Framed pictures lay stacked face down. He imagined his ol' man jus' takin' 'em off the wall, turnin' 'em down, an' shovin' 'em in there. With a glance at all the empty nails stickin' from the walls in the trailer, Davis realized how likely his imagination might jus' be. If the ol' man was anything more than stubborn he was simple an' straight forward.

Davis grabbed a handful of 'em an' turned 'em over one by one on the floor. His ol' man an' his momma standin' out front of some old place near the beach. He couldn't remember seein' his ol' man so young, but jus' as he imagined his momma's glow stole that sour-puss look on his face an' Davis was pretty sure after the photo the ol' man smiled. She was glowin'. Davis jus' stared at her for a minute, takin' it in. The next couple frames showed a baby swaddled in blankets an' two young, but tired faces. It was likely his brother, he knew. The older brother nobody talked 'bout much, the one Davis couldn't remember. Frame after frame, old photos of places an' parties with relatives he couldn't remember or maybe even never met. Jus' when Davis thought to stop, he turned one over an' saw them. It was his brother when he was about Davis' age now, standin' in front of a blue pickup – the same one he'd seen in the image in his mind the other day when he was rememberin' with his ol' man. Only what stole his breath wasn't how much his brother reminded him of him, his ball cap all lifted up with his hands buried in his jeans, but the girl beside him. A beautiful smile with a ponytail an' cut-off jeans. Allie.

Davis looked away, closed his eyes, shook his head, an' looked back again.

She was younger, his age, an' no less beautiful than she was today. She'd been his brother's girlfriend? His breath choked in his throat an' staggered out like a cough that decided to go down the wrong pipe, but that hadn't been the end of it. Beside 'em, on the other side of the truck, stood Liam King.

~*~

"What's that mean?" Mr. Allen asked. His eyes darted between the two men standin' in front of him, their hands tucked into the tactical vests –the same vests they'd worn when they raided the mechanic shop that mornin'.

Detective Barnett slid his hand across his wiry facial hair an' then fidgeted with his sunglasses folded in the flap beneath the large velcro patch that read *Sheriff's Deputy*.

"Well, we'd hoped to conduct the raid with everyone present, but of course, that's not always possible. Some folks jus' aren't gonna be there. Now, we got Compton an' quite a few of the bigger, heavier hitters our intel an' your information tol' us about, but the other two men, Chester Higgins an' John Buckingham, weren't there."

"So, yer sayin' they're still out there somewhere?"

"Yessir," the other deputy replied. "We've got patrols out trackin' Mr. Higgins' truck, an' we're canvasin' their frequented locations, but as for now we haven't found 'em. Is there any additional information you could give us to help?"

Mr. Allen shrugged. "So, do you thank they know 'bout the raid?"

"We haven't checked all the phone messages yet, but it's likely," the deputy replied.

"Even so, they're not gonna know who directly...," Detective Barnett began, but Mr. Allen interrupted.

"Yessir, they will! That's part of the problem. Has been for a lil' while now. Everyone in the shop's practically been waitin' on me to rat 'em out, an' here now the whole shop's shut down, they'll run straight for me without a blink, an' they're 'bout half-cocked enough to do somethin' stupid 'bout it, too. Look, my kid's stranded at home right now, an' I'm supposed to jus' go home? An' we're supposed to sleep tonight knowin' they're jus' a shotgun trigger away?"

"I understand, Sir. Is there anywhere y'all can stay 'til we get this sorted out?"

"Not really," Mr. Allen replied. "Ain't got any family 'round. An' even if there was, we're drivin' the same truck they're gonna know to follow. Cain't rightly jus' up an' disappear like they do in the movies, fellas."

"It's only a matter of time before we close in on 'em, Mr. Allen. We've got three cities patrollin' for these guys. My guess is they're more worried 'bout stayin' low than tyin' off any loose ends." Detective Barnett replied. "I'm not sayin' for certain, but I'm jus' sayin' it's a good chance."

"Sorry we don't have better news for ya, Mr. Allen, but we'll let you know as soon as we have 'em in custody, jus' to ease yer mind a bit. Between now an' then, we'll escort you home an' finish up some paperwork. There're still a few written statements we're gonna need you to sign."

Mr. Allen nodded and placed the wad of wire with the small microphone and box into the deputy's hand, then shook both their hands. While a big part of him was relieved at the thought of it all, an' so many bein' locked away, there was still that naggin' feelin' those knuckleheads weren't as clever as the deputies were given 'em credit.

"Oh," Detective Barnett added with a point to Deputy Johnson, rememberin' another detail, "an' don't forget to swing by the Mr. King's house an' thank him for lettin' us use his land to stage on."

"King's land?"

Deputy Johnson nodded.

"Yeah, the land behind the shop belonged to a local. Good young fella, best we could tell. Liam King, was it, Sir?"

Detective Barnett nodded.

"Anyhow, had to get permission by law to stage on it. Without his consent we'd 'ave had our hands tied for even longer waitin' on a judge order. He said he was familiar with the place, an' he knew some of the fellas had been up to no good for a few years now, but he hadn't known 'bout the drugs. Spoke highly of you though. Said y'all's families went way back. Made this whole process a lot smoother."

"Thank you, again, for your cooperation with all this," Detective Barnett added while Mr. Allen was still tryin' to wrap his head 'round it all. "Hope all this works out well for you an' yers. Deputy Johnson here will give you that escort home now."

~*~

Davis eased his bike up against the mossy oak in the front yard an' tried to shake the embarrassment away. How many folks had seen him ridin' it through Harrison, he wondered? It wasn't 'til he was almost at the front door he glanced around an' remembered an important detail that'd slipped his mind altogether. Why was he so worried how he'd look on a bike when even Liam King didn't have a truck?

Three quick raps on the door, an' he took a step back. When the door opened, he'd expected to see the sturdy fella fill the frame, but what he saw took his breath for a hot minute. Purple braids danced across her shoulders behind a set of golden eyes, her dark skin practically shinin' like the gulf.

Davis had to check the house again, scannin' the number to make sure it'd been the one he remembered.

"Can I help you?" she asked, jus' as confused as him.

"Uh. Yes ma'am. I thank so. I'm, uh, is this where Liam King lives?"

"Yeah, I bet you weren't ready for no black girl to answer the door, huh? Done got you all messed up."

"I, uh," Davis smiled when what she said finally made sense. "Is he home by any chance?"

"Nope. He's at work. Imma tell 'em you came by though, but Imma need to know who you is?"

"Davis...Davis Allen."

"Davis? He ain't never talked 'bout you, Mr. Allen. Where you from?"

"I'm from here. I mean, I live 'round 'ere."

"Okay, okay. Y'all go to church together?"

"No, ma'am."

"Y'all work together?"

"No, ma'am."

Huh... "So, I bet you all messed up why some black girl be answerin' his door, huh? I'm his baby momma."

Davis' mouth dropped open.

She laughed an' slapped her leg. "Yo face is fire! I'm messin', bruh. I'm messin'. He ain't got no kid or no girl. I'm jus' visitin' from outta town. We tight. He my boy. What you need, man?"

"I, uh, I jus' found somethin' an' I's wonderin' if he could help me answer some questions 'bout it."

"What's that? A picture?"

"Yeah, it's..."

"Okay! Yeah, that be Liam an' Allie. Okay, I see."

"You know Allie?"

"Yeah, we straight. She's sittin' my-boy Mr. Monte's gran-son, Travis. Yeah. But I don't know the other guy, yet. I ain't been in Harrison but a minute, right?"

"That's...my brother," Davis said.

"Okay, he cute. I see some resemblance."

Davis smirked. "Well, thank you Miss. I'll stop by later, or maybe he can call me? You gotta phone? I can leave you my number."

"I see you, playa. Tryna leave me your number all smooth. I say me an' Liam ain't nothin' an' now you tryna make yo move...okay!"

"I, uh..."

She laughed. "I'm jus' messin'. Here, write it down an' I'll make sure I tell him some lil' white boy stopped by tryna pick a fight wit him."

Davis laughed. "Naw, don't do that?"

"Yeah, he big, huh? I know you ain't tryna bump wit him. That's why I call him Superman. Man straight swoll, for real!"

Davis laughed again, shakin' his head. "Thank you, Miss..."

"Jewel," she said.

"Miss Jewel," he replied, slidin' his phone back in his pocket.

"Yeah, y'all be stayin' wit that *Miss* down here, for real. Imma tell him you stopped by Davis. Davis? Mississippi be full of all these las' names as firs' names, too. It's tight though. You look like a Davis...or a Brad. You could be a Brad, too."

"Davy?" a voice interrupted from behind them. Neither one of them had seen the Jeep pull up in the distance. Davis turned to see Allie standin' with her hands tucked in her jeans.

"Hi, Miss Jewel," she said a lil' sweeter than she'd said his name, but Davis figured he'd earned that in a way, what with the party at the river an' the fightin' an' all.

"Hey girl! We 'bouts to have a party up in here. Er'body's comin' by."

Allie smiled. "Is Liam 'round, Miss Jewel?"

"Nah, that's what I's tellin' Mr. Allen here. He at work. Why? You straight? Travis be aight?"

Allie waved her hand dismissin' Jewel's worry. "Naw, everythang's good, jus' stoppin' by to chitchat."

Jewel smiled an' the sight seemed to catch Allie by surprise. She smiled back. Was she blushin' a lil'?

"I'm finna charge this clown takin' all his messages. Liam gonna get a phone wit me aroun', for real. I ain't gonna be his secretary every day!"

"Good luck with that," Allie said. "That boy ain't never wanted a phone."

They laughed and said goodbyes, but as Davis an' Allie started to make their way back down the gravel drive, Davis cleared his throat.

"I'm sorry 'bout the other night, an' about the fightin'. There's lots of thangs goin' on right now, an' it's all sort of..."

"I know, Davy," Allie interrupted. "You might not believe me, but I've seen this all before, an' it's like watchin' an ol' movie again. I love Mr. Allen, but he's got these *habits*, an' people 'round him ain't much to shake a stick at, if you know what I mean."

Davis nodded, not entirely sure what she meant by 'habits', or how she even knew heads or tails of any of it, but he could certainly agree with her view of Cheesy an' Buckwheat.

"I meant what I said the other day when I gave you the bag. You're better than that life, Davy. Don't waste it. Don't drown yerself in it. You'll get lost. An' those girls an' the whole party scene, I mean, I know it's fun, but there's another side to it y'all ain't thinkin' clearly 'bout right now."

Davis fidgeted with the picture in his back pocket, wonderin' if he should tug it out. One voice shouted *don't*, but the other moved his hand the rest of the way to offer it to her.

"Where'd you find this?" she asked.

"In a chest. That's why I came here to Liam, to ask him what it all meant. Were you two, I mean, did you an' him?"

At first, Davis could tell Allie either wasn't sure how to answer, or maybe whether she should. After a breath or two, she finally nodded. "Me an' Kenny were a thing. We were *the* thing."

"Wow," Davis said. "I...It all makes sense now. I couldn't figure out why y'all knew me an' my mom and ol' man, but now..."

"We were all pretty close for a while, our dads an' moms. 'Course mine were a lot older than yours, but they all went to church together an'...."

"*My* ol' man?" Davis echoed. "Church?"

Allie smiled. "Oh yeah. Yeah, an' yer momma used to play the piano, too. She even gave me lessons whenever I'd sit still long enough."

"We'd get together after church on Sundays an' have lunches, laughin' an' carryin' on with Liam an' his folks. They were the pastors back then before they moved to Haiti. The three of us were inseparable."

"Hey, you headed home now?" she asked, pointin' at his bike. Embarrassed reached a whole new level to Davis then, but as usual Allie didn't seem to care 'bout those sorts of things. If there was a record somewhere, she was definitely the prettiest thing Walmart ever clothed.

"Yeah,"

"Toss in it the back of the Jeep an' I'll give you a ride so we can chat. How's that?"

"Aight," he replied. "I'd like that a lot."

26

THURSDAY THUNDERSTORM

THURSDAY AFTERNOON

Took a ride. Be back later.

Bob Allen sat the note down an' reached in his back pocket to look at his phone. Sure enough, the boy'd tried to call an' message him, but for some reason he hadn't seen or heard not a one. He sighed, annoyed, half-watchin' the Sheriff Deputy back outta the red clay drive an' toss a hand up in a wave. He couldn't count how many times him an' Det. Barnett said they were sure as shootin' Cheesy an' Buckwheat would be hauled-in by the end of the day, but there's still somethin' naggin' at the back of his mind 'bout it all. And he's pretty sure that naggin' wouldn't stop 'til he got the call lettin' him know for certain.

~*~

"Y'ought to head on home," Mr. Montgomery said with a nod toward the clouds bulkin' up beyond the islands. "It's gettin' that season an' that time of day for a good gully-washer."

"You sure?" Liam asked. "Still another hour yet an' we've got a crowd."

"Yeah, but you know they'll be clearin' out before too long, an' we cain't do nothin' 'round here when the rain comes."

Liam nodded. "Tell my buddy I said hey."

"Tell him yerself. I's thinkin' 'bout runnin' him by the house later an' sittin' for a lil' bit."

"That'd be great! I'll get the grill goin', too."

"Need anything?"

"Nah, jus' some more mouths."

"Travis will want his Crawtaters,"

"That makes two of us," Liam said. "Oh, an' I bet Jewels might like 'em, too. I don't know that she's had 'em."

Mr. Montgomery smiled at the mention of her name.

"Aight, son. We'll see ya then."

The gully-washer came quicker than they usually do. Liam had grown up watchin' 'em roll through the fields like clockwork 'bout the same time every day, it seemed. They didn't last long, but the rain fell in sheets an' the drops sounded 'bout the size of a five-gallon bucket's worth crashin' down. Soon as they passed, the sun leapt back out an' seemed to shine harder an' hotter than ever. That's when the humidity exploded an' the gulf coast felt like a sauna 'til sunset.

He picked up his pace, an' even cut a few more corners than usual, tryin' ta beat it home, but the sound of the whoosh crawlin' through the woods in the distance, an' the cool, whippin' breeze jus' ahead of it, tol' him he was gonna get soaked. And he did. Took 'bout three seconds an' he would've thought a shower might've used less water.

Wasn't but a minute later, he heard a truck easin' up behind him, slowin' down beside the road where he's walkin'. He glanced over half-expectin' to see Mr. Montgomery laughin', shakin' his head, but what he saw nearly knocked him over.

An off-white pick-up rolled to a stop an' jus' beyond the blindin' wall of water, he saw the driver lean down across the cabin an' lift the latch on the door. Mr. Allen hollered an' tol' him to get in with a wave. Liam didn't hesitate. He wanted to. But there's somethin' 'bout the thought of turnin' down any act of kindness, no matter how odd it felt, that'd always unsettled Liam. Besides, to turn him down or keep him waitin' while Liam tried to make sense of it all seemed more foolish than standin' out in a gully-wash.

"Thought you'd take a swim, huh?" he said.

"Yessir. Should-a brought soap," Liam replied.

"I'm drivin' 'round lookin' for Davis. His truck's all banged up, so he took the ol' bike somewhere an' he's likely to look like you right 'bout now. Headed home?"

"If it ain't floated away by the time we get there."

"Yours won't. Mine might," Mr. Allen replied. "Front yard looks like a lake this time of year."

"Could always do some front yard worm fishin', I guess."

It came out as soon as the memory entered his mind. They'd been 'bout ten, him an' Kenny, when a tropical storm came through Harrison an' left the yards flooded for days. Mr. Allen propped 'em up on his front porch with two reels. Told 'em to try an' catch the earthworms.

Liam didn't know why he said it. It jus' sort of came out, an' as soon as it did, he regretted it. All he could do was stare at his lap, wonderin' what might happen next.

Then, Bob Allen laughed.

"That's one hell-of-a-memory," he said between the fits. "You'd 'ave thought I took y'all deep sea fishin'."

Liam was beside himself. He smiled, but still couldn't bring himself to look for too long at Mr. Allen for fear of the memories –an' the regrets. Regrets he knew shouldn't be there anymore.

"It was...to us."

"Goes to show some of the best memories are the ones y'ain't gotta pay for, I reckon."

"Amen to that," Liam said reflexively, but then immediately regretted that too. He shouldn't 'ave said anything churchy either.

But jus' like before, if Mr. Allen noticed, if there's any bad blood between 'em, Liam couldn't tell. It was a surreal feelin', like he's dreamin' or Mr. Allen wasn't himself. What felt like an hour passed in a minute or two of silence while Liam swiped more an' more water from his hair an' face.

"Good thang these seats ain't all clothy. It'd take a store full of towels to mop you up."

Liam chuckled. "Yeah, I appreciate it. Lord knows I'm gonna go through a few inside the front door."

Lord knows? Seriously! What's wrong with me? Liam's mind kept screamin' at him. Was he tryin' to set Mr. Allen off?

"Yeah, that's for sure," he replied. "Guess that ain't no different than when we used to 'ave to hose y'all off some days before we'd even let ya inside to take showers, is it?"

Liam remembered those deep Mississippi ditches, the red clay, an' the roads he an' Kenny would carve in 'em, racin'

Matchbox cars back an' forth in ankle deep water kickin' crawdad mounds whenever they weren't catchin' 'em. How many shirts an' jeans had they ruined playin' in the red dirt, he wondered?

"Heard you gave the deputies permission to use some land," he said suddenly, catchin' Liam by surprise.

"Yessir. They, uh, stopped by the other mornin' when I was out walkin' it."

"That's 'bout 15 acres, ain't it? When did yer folks buy all that?"

"Yessir. Well, it's jus' a lil' under ten. They didn't. I bought it jus' a few years back. I'd been savin' for a while an' it was burnin' a hole in my pocket."

"You an' Kenny wouldn't shut up 'bout that land, if I recall."

Liam nodded. "Yessir. We had some dreams 'bout openin' shops an' all sorts of nonsense."

"So you followed through, huh?"

"Lots of memories there. Couldn't see 'em disappear into someone else's yard, I suppose. Saw the sign one day an' a friend helped me bargain the price. Mr. Montgomery always said buyin' land was the best investment a young fella could make, so…"

"Yeah, wise fella. I miss ol' Monte. How's he been?"

"Havin' him an' Travis over tonight to do some grillin'. You an' Davy could come, if you ain't got nothin' goin' on."

"I'll, uh, we'll see. I need to find that squirt, first. See what he's got goin' on."

He was nicely declinin', Liam knew. Too much friendliness too quick after so long felt awkward, an' the silence that followed proved it.

"Anyhow," Mr. Allen finally said, "I'm glad I caught ya takin' yer weekly bath. I wanted to thank ya for lettin' 'em on yer land to do all that this mornin'. Took a lot of bad folks outta Harrison today. Deputy said without your permission, it could've tied things up for a few extra days. An' like you saw at the church the other day, things were gettin' a might hairy between the folks who were doin' the dealin' an' those who weren't."

"Here I jus' thought y'all's fightin' like most Mississippi folks —over whose truck was better."

Mr. Allen chuckled.

"All this mess is gonna close the shop though, ain't it?" Liam asked.

"Yeah," he replied, an' Liam didn't miss his tone shift a bit more somber. "A catch-22, I reckon."

"Took a lot o' grit ta make a trade like that," Liam said. Mr. Allen merely nodded, unsure how to take the compliment. They took the bend by the bar, past the spot where Liam found Jewels, an' it wasn't too long before Mr. Allen glanced up in the rear view mirror an' his brow knotted up, an' he breathed an annoyed sigh. Liam leaned forward an' caught a glimpse of the sight from the side mirror.

The green Chevy. Same one that'd been in the church parkin' lot the other day.

"These fellas, again? Thought they'd 'ave been rounded up this mornin with the rest of 'em?"

"They lucked out. I suppose they've been hidin' out back behind the bar outta sight, but I reckon their luck's 'bout to change," Mr. Allen said passin' Liam his phone. "What ya say you make a phone call for me?"

~*~

Allie went through the light at the four-way an' Davis naturally turned his head toward his house, but she didn't turn. The thought didn't bother him –ridin' 'round with Allie talkin' 'bout his brother an' how things had been– so he jus' went with it 'til she rounded the bend, past the *Hidden Drive* sign, an' turned onto the gravel drive up to her house. She pulled the Jeep clear up to the shed an' nodded toward the door.

"Got somethin' to show ya," she said.

They glanced over their shoulder to the clouds rollin' in, stealin' the light lil' by lil', but that didn't seem to stop her from openin' the shed door an' leadin' the way in. Davis watched as she fidgeted with the tarp, unhookin' the rubber straps, an' liftin' the front 'til it rolled back the length of the hood an' half the driver-side door.

It was the blue truck in the picture, the one from his memory.

"This was Kenny's," she said. She shoved her hands in her jeans an' nudged the front tire with her shoe. "Liam an' I had it fixed up before his folks wouldn't let him come 'round anymore."

Davis imagined he looked like a fish out of water, but all he could do was slide his hand across the hood. For some reason it made him feel like he was seein' his brother, though he couldn't remember a genuine memory he had of him. This had been the truck the wreck happened in, he knew. But it looked new.

"Does it run?"

"Yep," she said with a sharp nod. "I'll start her up every once in a while, an' take Kelli out in it. She'll sit on my lap an' we'll jus' coast 'round back yonder, past the garage in the fields where momma's garden used to be, near the woods."

"Why'd you...I mean,"

"Why'd we fix it?" Allie asked. "I think it's 'cause we missed him. But then part of me thinks it's 'cause of how much it might mean...to Kelli."

Davis stopped lookin' at the truck then when a baseball-of-a-knot filled his throat. All he could do was stare, first at the truck, then slowly at Allie.

"Kelli?"

Allie nodded.

"She's your..."

"Daughter," Allie said. "Kenny's daughter. Your niece, Davy. You're an uncle."

He fought to ask more questions, but the baseball lodged itself in there good.

"Does my ol' man know?"

Allie nodded. "It was a lot of drama back in the day. Got both our families shamed. We thought we were in love, an' I think we were too for a time, but things have a way of changin' kids, Davy, an' that's who we were –kids. Sure, we thought we knew all sorts of things, like you an' yer buddies down by the river, but truth was we were lettin' our hearts an' our emotions lead us where our brains hadn't planned out yet. We weren't thinkin' past the here an' now."

"I have a niece," Davis said. "I'm an uncle."

"Which is good enough a reason as any to get your act right. Cain't rightly spend time with her if you're actin' like a kid."

Davis rubbed his hand on the hood again as he looked at the picture, wonderin' what life would've been like with Kenny in it. Allie finally cleared her throat an' crossed her arms over her chest with a slight shiver as a cool breeze rushed into the shed. Rain was comin'. They could smell it. She nodded toward the truck.

"But now I'm wonderin' if the reason we fixed 'er up was so you could 'ave her."

Davis shook his head, clearin' out the cobwebs. "Me?"

Allie swiped the backside of her hand across her cheek, wipin' a few tears away Davis hadn't even noticed had fallen.

"We had Kenny. We have the memories you didn't get to. I suppose if havin' somethin' like this might fill a hole somewhere, it'd be worth it. It'd make us cryin' an' fixin' it up all those days have a purpose other than lettin' it sit every day under a tarp."

Davis wanted to say no, but he didn't. He couldn't. Only one thought bothered him.

"What about Kelli an' her memories?"

"Well," Allie said with a shrug, "I suppose if we do things right from here on out, she'll have a Gran-dad an' an uncle to give her new ones, won't she?"

27

AFTER THE RAIN

THURSDAY AFTERNOON

The green Chevy pressed so close Liam could see both their faces clearly in the side mirror, an' with the rain still fallin' in sheets that was sayin' somethin'.

"Think they'll bump us? Run us off the road?"

"Better off knowin' what a squirrel might do."

They passed Liam's house, an' he was thankful. He didn't want Jewels dragged into anything, or to have to see anything dangerous. Deputy Johnson said he was 'bout ten to fifteen minutes out, which meant a lot of drivin' an' some doublin' back, but with the looks of things those two didn't seem like the chasin' sort, and the way the passenger was fidgetin' with somethin' in his lap, Liam swallowed hard at what it might mean if they kept it up for too much longer.

Liam didn't know a lot 'bout what was goin' on at the shop, but he'd heard 'drugs', an' with that whole scene money, guns, an' blood often followed, an' the thought didn't ease his mind much. Mr. Allen tried to keep his cool as best

216

he could with the storm carryin' on. He couldn't stop for fear of what they might do behind him, but he slowed down to make sure they could whiz through the intersections without endangerin' anybody. Thankfully, everybody else was a bit smarter than them, an' were likely waitin' it out instead of drivin' in it, which made things a bit easier when Mr. Allen took a hard left past the church an' pressed down the pedal toward the outskirts, near the highway.

"Good idea gettin' toward the highway," Liam said.

"Figured the deputy might be headin' this-a-way."

"Think they'll try an' pass once the road opens?"

"Might," Mr. Allen said, an' Liam didn't miss the twinge of a sound in his voice that added *'but I hope not'* to the end of it.

Before they could slow down at the second intersection past Marco's, they swerved around an' tried to pull up beside 'em. Mr. Allen hit the gas an' rushed through with more than a few folks glarin' from the windows of Fancy's. It wasn't too long before the sickly green Chevy jerked wildly to the side an' sped up, tryin' to get alongside 'em in oncoming traffic.

"They might have a gun," Liam said. "Saw him messin' with somethin' in his lap."

"I's afraid of that. Sorry I snatched you up in this mess,"

"You kiddin'? Before this the most excitin' thing I did was have a jalapeno with lunch."

They shared an uneasy chuckle before Liam added, "Better there's somebody 'round to witness it, so it ain't jus' yer word against theirs."

The truck was almost even with 'em when another set of headlights came into view from the opposite direction. The road hadn't widened yet, which meant they'd need to rush past or fall back behind, an' by the looks of things they didn't have the secon' thought as an' option.

Mr. Allen pushed on the brakes an' let 'em dart past an' over in time to see the other car whiz by. It was a Jeep. Allie's jeep. And for a split second, he could see her an' the passenger notice the trucks, an' he wasn't sure, but he thought they saw one another, too.

"Sir," Liam said with a point over his shoulder. "I think that was Allie in that jeep back there, an' I think Davy was with her."

They both glanced back to see the brake lights turn into headlights as the Jeep turned around in a driveway.

Mr. Allen mumbled what Liam could tell was likely a few choice curse words at the sight of them doublin' back, ones he no longer chose to mumble a few seconds later when the green Chevy shoved on the brakes an' they nearly rear-ended 'em. Had a car been in the oncoming lane, they'd have crashed straight into 'em, but a quick jerk took 'em around an' past.

How much further 'til the deputy's here, Liam wondered as the thought of Allie an' Davy gettin' caught up in the mess irked him more with each passin' second, an' the bend near Allie's house came into view. Liam never came this way anymore. Never needed to. It'd been so familiar to him at one point in his life: a daily ride to an' from school, back an' forth on the weekends. There wasn't a day passed for more than two years when he an' Kenny weren't huggin' the curve around the bend, rushin' to practice or to Allie.

Then, after Kenny died, the long walks out there had been almost as routine, smoothin' paths underfoot through the woods and by the river. Lots of thoughts got lost in those woods. Only a few made it to be scribbled down in a journal later, but those were the safe ones an' the questions.

The wildest ones came when no one could read them; the thoughts of Allie he'd always imagined —the feelin' of holdin' her hand in his; what it might be like to touch her cheek right before he kissed her, like they do in the movies, and even the sound of her voice tellin' him she loved him. He left those in the trees for the leaves to hold, day after day.

But that felt like an eternity ago. Another life between different people, ones yesterday taught him had changed so much, yet so little in the flash of a decade. With a glance in the side mirror, at the headlights creepin' up closer, Liam felt the sunlight tricklin' through the leaves down on the path while he walked like it was yesterday. Nearer. Nearer. Then, suddenly gone.

At the sight of the deputy's lights, the green Chevy slammed on the brakes. Mr. Allen darted to the left, into the oncoming lane again, only this time the driver had anticipated it. He swerved and drove the front end of his truck into the passenger side of Pearly. Both trucks slid on the wet road at the bend. Pearly's back end hit the gravel on the roadside first. Mr. Allen tried to turn it back toward the Chevy, but then quickly gave up an' spun the wheel toward the ditch when they started to slide. He'd 'ave corrected it if they'd 'ave been on ice, or if the ditch had been a front yard, but none of that mattered when the Chevy followed 'em, an' continued to shove 'em as far as it could.

They hit the ditch side by side, still slidin' 'til both left side tires disappeared down into it. Then, the Chevy planted itself clear into the passenger side an' shoved it down, then over, as it flipped.

~*~

Allie screamed. Not a scary movie type scream, or any other sort of fake ones Davis had heard his entire life. This was a deep one. A real one. One from the soul. All he could think to do was lean forward an' reach to unbuckle his seat belt, but the Jeep hadn't stopped yet. So, all he *could* do was wait in horror while Allie slowed down an' pulled back into the drive. The deputies made it to the scene as soon as they did, yankin' Cheesy an' Buckwheat off an' onto the ground by the roadside as they climbed from the passenger side door of the cab. The driver side was buried into the passenger side of Pearly, a mucky mixture of colors.

The secon' deputy placed handcuffs on 'em, while Deputy Johnson an' Davis fought an' scraped 'round the wreckage for a way into Pearly's cab. The windshield was a spiderweb of a mess, half-hangin'. The back window was pinched at the hood, barely more than a regular sized window now that the Chevy had squished it like blueberry.

He could hear somethin' inside —some sort of a ruckous, wigglin' an' squirmin' an' the like— but with the rain fallin' in sheets all 'round his face, hittin' the shattered glass, an' with no doors to open, Davis didn't have many options.

"Pop!" he screamed, pressin' his face as close as he could to get a glance inside.

"Mr. Allen?" Deputy Johnson shouted. "Young man, stay back!"

"It's my dad. My dad's in there!" Davis growled. He yanked his hat off an' put his hand inside it to protect it while he grabbed at the fringes of the rear window glass an' tried to pry it off with little success.

Ms. Luanne was on the front porch, one hand on the rail, the other over her mouth.

"Can we pull the truck off? We gotta pull the truck off!" Davis shouted over the rain.

"I've called it in, son. Help is comin'! They'll know what to do safely. If we try an' do somethin' it might make it worse."

"That'll take too long! We've gotta...we can get a chain or a rope an' pull it off. Then, maybe we can climb through the passenger side..." Davis replied, but the Deputy wasn't listenin' anymore. He rushed back to the windshield, yanked his over-shirt off an' wrapped it around the busted part of the windshield, then yanked. Half came off.

And Davis wished it hadn't.

He saw 'em then, the ol' man an' Liam. His big arms were still wrapped around him where they'd pulled him back, away from the door as it slammed into the ditch and buried itself clear through the steerin' wheel. Liam had been wearin' his seat belt, an' that's what'd held him upright to snatch the ol' man away, but the old truck's lap belts weren't the same as the ones in Allie's jeep. The cabin collapsed around Liam, folded 'round him like a metal taco as he bent sidelong. The ol' man groaned an' stirred, whimperin', his head a mangled mess of blood. Before Davis could make heads or tails of it, the secon' deputy arrived an' pulled him back. Deputy Johnson wasted no time crawlin' in as far as he could, to help his ol' man.

At first, Davis fought the deputy, but then he saw Allie comin' 'round the truck, an' he knew she couldn't see. She shouldn't see.

"Okay. Okay," he said to the deputy. "Stop *her!* Don't let her see!"

They both rushed to hold her back an' the sight of 'em rushin' with their hands out put even more of a fight in her. It took both of 'em to keep her from makin' it to the front of Pearly. She screamed an' punched, her tears minglin' with the rain, 'til all Davis could do was wrap his arms around her an' squeeze her into the biggest hug he could manage. In a way he'd been able to protect her like Liam did his ol' man, and somewhere deep down a lil' part of Davis died there, too, with the sounds of Allie's cries fillin' his ears. They'd echo in his memory for the rest of his life, especially those days when the gulf storms brought the rain down in sheets an' he'd find himself trapped out in it.

The minutes felt like hours waitin' on the firetrucks an' the ambulance to arrive. By then, the ditch was crawlin' with men tearin' the truck apart to get to 'em, an' the gully-washer had passed, replaced by lil' breaks 'ere an' there in the clouds an' the onset of what'd become another miserably hot evenin' 'til an orange an' pink wispy sunset intermixed with a deep blue sky an' what remained of dark gray clouds sailin' off north toward Hattiesburg.

SUNDAY MORNING

Here he was, *back*.

Only this wasn't the 'back' he'd hoped he'd find. Not like this.

An' you knew that, he thought into the darkness of the early morning. *You knew all this would happen long before I even asked for it.*

He didn't feel like thinkin' 'bout it anymore. He could still hear the squealin' of the tires, the jar, the slam of the whole left side crashin' into the ditch, lodgin' there with the sound of the rainwater an' the muck welcomin' the tires. Then, the scrapin' an' bitin' 'round him, like a metal monster took hold of him in its jaws, ready to chomp.

"Jesus!" he'd heard him yell.

Before he knew what'd happened those big arms yanked him back from the window as the ground quickly made its way toward 'em an' the truck on top of 'em pressed down harder jus' fer spite. No sooner had he yanked him back from bein' pinned between the steerin' column an' the ground, the whole ride stopped an' everything went quiet.

If I'd 'ave known you's gonna bring me back here, I wouldn't 'ave asked, he thought.

But unlike all the other times, he didn't get a reply. He tried to remember the night he'd finally hit the bottom –the night he wanted the change. It felt like a year ago since that day. How many times had he thought about the changes, the days that brought confusion an' chaos, only to end the way they did? Sure, the little victories 'ere an' there had been nice, but all-in-all, that feelin' –those memories– would haunt him. They'd haunt anyone.

Jus' when he'd had 'bout enough pain-thinkin', an' started to yank the sheets aside, he saw him again in the back of his mind. He's a kid again, hootin' an' hollerin', runnin' 'round the yard with Kenny, playin' God knows what, sticks in their hands, stabbin' bad guys. No low hangin' tree branch was safe, an' if fire ant hills could die they'd 'ave committed mass genocide at leas' once a week.

Then, he saw him again, soakin' wet, sittin' in the truck beside him wearin' a smile, talkin' an' jokin', man-to-man. As short-lived as it was, a piece of those moments wove 'round in his mind 'til he felt like there's a third fella sittin' between 'em on that God-awful day. Kenny would've had a few laughs at both their expenses, what with him bein' a wet mess, an' the ol' man out scourin' for Davy like a mother hen.

Quit bein' a sissy, the boy'll turn up, he might've said. *What's he gonna do, get wet? Wreck his bike? Scrape his knee? Tell'm rub some dirt on it!*

There'd 'ave been some story 'bout one of the dozen or so times he'd told the two of 'em the same things whenever they came boo-hooin' 'bout some bloody knuckles or a busted lip. How many times had he hollered *"ain't no cryin' in baseball"* whenever a line drive popped up all wonky an' caught one of 'em in the gut, or died laughin' when it snuck up between the knees.

"Hey Kenny, you okay?" The ol' man would holler from the stands in his highest pitch girly voice, all the dads laughin' along while the moms jus' shook their heads.

Or *"Nice toss, Leah! Got one of 'em in mens?"* whenever he didn't quite make the throw to first in time to get the runner out.

All he could do was lay in the bed an' cry as the memories came, one after the other.

Almost there, the voice said again. *Keep movin' forward.*

28

THE READING

SUNDAY AFTERNOON

Suits an' ties made everything worse. The fact it was a pretty day, with the sunlight siftin' between the leaves an' a cool spring breeze shufflin' from shade to shade didn't seem fair at first thought, but then the longer folks lingered, the more Davis appreciated the space to get out an' away from it all —to take a walk down by the lil' creek under the mossy oaks.

His hands stayed buried in his pockets. It's the only place they felt right. He's tired of meetin' folks; tired of shakin' hands an' givin' a grim nod whenever someone would start a lil' story 'bout how they hadn't seen him in years, or how much he looked like his brother or his ol' man when he was younger. Things folks would never say any other day if they saw him at Marco's or Fancy's. Truth was it jus' seemed fake. It all seemed put-on an' in a way he wondered if they were jus' sort of tryin' to make up for what they all felt like they should've said back when things were different. How would things be if people treated one another like that, he wondered?

Allie was there holdin' Kelli's hand with Ms. Luanne not too far away. Everyone treated them the same, but they seemed to be takin' it better than he was. A big part of Davis hoped they could all stand 'round one another eventually, but the more people came, the more he had to stay away. He'd never been to a funeral; at least, one he could remember. Kat, Paige, an' Cora Lynn were there with tissues in hand, their faces red an' swollen, a sight no amount of make-up could hide. After a lil' while Allie placed Kelli's hand in Ms. Luanne's an' walked away. Davis tried to make his way to her, but when he found her, she was standin' with her arms around another guy, holdin' him while he rocked back an' forth in his chair.

"If I'd been there, I'd 'ave saved him Allie-girl," he said.

"I know, but he'd 'ave been mad at ya," she said.

"Mad?" he replied, breathlessly like he'd been punched. He stopped rockin'. "How come? Liam weren't never mad at me before. Never."

"'Cause then he wouldn't be with Jesus, buddy," the ol' man on the other side of him added.

"But...but..." he said, rockin' again.

"An' we both know Jesus is the only person he'd rather be with than you, huh?" Allie said.

"Yeah, I'm his best friend, but Jesus is his best, best friend," he replied. "That's what he'd say, huh, Allie-girl? Jesus was his best, best friend."

"Yep," she said. She didn't even try to stop the tears.

~*~

A few chosen people stood an' gave speeches, sayin' a bunch of nice things an' talkin' 'bout people Jewels didn't know. Everyone talked 'bout Liam like they'd jus' spent the day wit' him yesterday. It reminded her how girls be actin' when some boy died back in Indy, an' suddenly they's seein' one another on the side. They wasn't, but they'd stay fakin' 'cause they liked the drama. Everybody stayed actin' like Liam used to roll wit everybody, an' they was all tight 'bout to hang tha' weekend or somethin'. As if they all hadn't been trash talkin' him only days before. Even the pastor stood up actin' like he hadn't jus' been all ratchety, jankin' Liam 'round an' finessin' his name.

All she could do was sit by Tamra an' Angel an' they husbands with her arms crossed in front of her, swallowed by the sweater he'd bought her. Mr. Monte came by an' so did Allie, even Davis made his way eventually. Others tried, but Jewels didn't play games. She couldn't. There was somethin' 'bout faces she couldn't stand, an' how so many folks whinin' an' gettin' hugged on for no good reason were wearin' two of 'em. She'd been to more funerals an' graves than weddin's an' birthday parties combined, an' she always felt the same at every one. People be likin' attention, always tryna make it 'bout dem.

After a lot of the talkin' stopped, an' the silence grew like an' unseen weight, a woman came up to the front to play a song on the piano while another woman Jewels didn't know was gonna sing. By then, she'd heard enough.

Jewels stood up, tears floodin' her cheeks. Some folks started to mumble, but Tamra stood up an' crossed her arms with an uplifted brow for someone to challenge her 'til she glared the gossips into silence. Then, she nodded for Jewels to uncoil what lay wrapped in her sweater sleeves like a heartfelt present. It was Liam's journal.

"He'd go on runs early in the mornin' an' leave this by the back porch open where he'd been writin' in it," she said in a hushed voice, tryin' to work up the boldness to speak through the tears a lil' louder as she did. "He knew I'd sneak a peak every now an' then, but I don't think he knew I stayed readin' this thing. See, Mr. King wasn't jus' some boy y'all be knowin' who was all good but then got all sneaky when nobody was lookin', like some o' these girls 'round here. I'm finna show you who Mr. King was. Who he *really* was."

She opened to a recent page, cleared her throat, and started to read.

I had these thoughts the other day when I's walkin' to the river to meet Travis an' find out who his sitter was. Jewels says she knows me, an' I know her, but I cain't for the life of me figure out who she thinks she is that I should be so quick to jump at her. She swears up an' down I ought ta marry her, an' that I love her. That girl is somethin' else! But, I guess Harrison ain't all that big. Truth is I might know her from 'round somewhere. Probably went to school together when we's kids. Life had been so much simpler then —those summer nights that never seemed to end. Sit in class, play ball, laugh, joke, go to church, then laugh an' joke some more. The days blended to years; everyday felt like an eternity, and every year didn't really matter —not really. It was the newness of it all. When we were young, everything was new and uncharted like the paths in the woods, and we were the trailblazers. Excitement buzzed with every great thing an' there wasn't anyone 'round for miles to tell us heads or tails of any of it. Just us. But then eventually the big circle of life started to wind around without anyone expectin' it to, or noticin' it, an' suddenly the jars and bumps in the road shook the newness right outta things.

Things happen.

Mistakes are made an' cain't nobody unmake 'em. Hearts are hurt. Sure, folks get sorry 'bout things an' try to hop back on the new trails, again —to keep pressin' ahead to the next fun, excitin' thing, but no matter how hard ya try it jus' ain't new anymore —it ain't the same. The circle's done, an' ya start over again. Only this time, it ain't as excitin' cause you've done seen all these things before.

That's when life gets hard an' ya gotta make a choice. Do ya let go of the taste of the newness an' embrace the thought of livin' an' learnin', or do ya scramble an' try to cling to the old flavors o' things secretly hopin' they'll come back if ya jus' try hard enough? I've watched folks struggle an' let go, fightin' in their own ways with the future an' what everything meant. Some didn't want to grow up, others did but weren't sure why 'til it was too late to even think about goin' back to the simpler times. By then, it was too late. Sure, mistakes had been made, but there'd still be plenty of fun an' laughs an' life to love on the other side of 'em too, but not everyone viewed things that-a-way.

I know I didn't for a while.

Some folks won't let ya mess up an' clean up, then enjoy the ride before ya mess up again. They'll watch ya mess up, an' before you can clean up, they seem bound an' determined to hurt folks —to cut 'em so deep they wouldn't even want to try for fear of messin' everything up again, much less ridin'. To them, that was called 'bein' an adult' an' takin' responsibility.

But I know better now.

Sure, bein' responsible is important an' jus' as necessary in life as the next thing, but not at the expense of wallerin' in the failures, or bein' kicked back into the mud hole when you're on the way out. Folks should be there with hands ready. Folks should be there to give 'em that unapologetic nod that shows 'em what they did sure was boneheaded, but that doesn't mean life is over. Not for a youngin'.

Folks should've been there for us. An' I'm gonna live the rest of my life rememberin' to be there for others, even if it means gettin' a little muddy to help others out of the hole.

"Tha's why he couldn't let me go. Tha's why he couldn't let me down," Jewel said. "It was the thought of all dem times people be cuttin' each other off an' stompin' each other when they's down, like they ain't never been there before too or somethin'. People be hatin' an' actin' like er'body else cain't make no mistakes, but they stay makin' 'em, an' expectin' er'body jus' keep walkin' like they ain't see it or somethin'."

Jewel wiped the tears from her face.

"But Superman wasn't like that. He didn't quit on nobody. Not even me. Mr. Allen," she said suddenly, an' in the back the ol' man lifted his head from where it'd hung all day, facin' the floor. "There's a lot in this journal 'bout you an' Kenny, an' he didn't quit on you neither. Tha' boy stayed prayin' for you. He stayed wrecked thinkin' he'd hurt y'all in a way nobody'd ever be able to forgive him. But we walked an' talked on a daily, an' I don't be knowin' for real what y'all was talkin' 'bout before the accident, but I know he was happy jus' to be wit you, talkin' to you."

"Mr. Monte, you my man! What you thought an' said stayed on his mind all day, e'ry day. He stayed listenin' to God an' you, one hundred percent. Facts. And don't nobody mess wit his best friend, Travis, too. 'Cause Liam gonna stitch you up on top a Ferris Wheel, huh Travis? 'Member dat?"

"He got you good, huh, Jewels?"

"Yeah, he did!"

"Allie-girl," she said, an' what lil' giggles intermingled with tears hushed once again at the sound of her name. "You prolly gonna need to check wit Momma-King first, but I think you should 'ave dis. Girl, I could open this thang to any page an' if your name *ain't* on it, I'd be shocked, for real. He taught me so much 'bout what it means to think 'bout people, but not jus' 'bout 'em, for 'em. Like, he stayed thinkin' for people an' how their situations could be better in a hot minute. He was all up on some positive. It was like he was prayin' with his words for er'body, 'specially you. Mr. King didn't love you, girl. Folks finna say love for er-thang. They be talkin' 'bout cars an' songs, teams, an' hot fries sayin' love. Naw. Imma say there's a word out there somewhere means more than *love*, an' tha's how my man, Liam felt 'bout you, girl."

"But you already know," Jewels said. It was then she couldn't hold 'em back anymore, an' her tears poured out like a flood. Her shoulders shook violently, but all she could do was shake her head. "Both of y'all stayed knowin' this word that's more than love forever, reachin' out y'all souls an' holdin' one another every day even though y'all never held one another like dat in ya arms. I can see it now like a movie in my mind. He tol' me one time to never give my heart away to some boy unless he was a Godly man. An' other than him, I don't know what a Godly man looks like, but for real – *bet!* –I'm finna wait 'til I find me one who I can find that word wit like dat. Then, I be stretchin' my soul out to hold him forever like you."

"He ran every Monday mornin' an' mailed dem letters to you, an' walked on that land he bought wonderin' what'd it'd be like wit you. He even made me walk it once, too –all poked up with vines, bugs all crawlin' up in my hair. Yeah, he prolly thought it was funny, too, but I ain't salty. Tha's my Superman, y'all. An' I don't know a lot 'bout Jesus other than what Mr. King taught me, an' that He saved me from my sins an' hell, but what I do know is He a thief to me right now, 'cause He done stole Mr. King from me an' I wasn't ready, y'all. I wasn't ready."

29

MOVIN' FORWARD

SUNDAY AFTERNOON

The ol' man hadn't said much since the wreck, an' Davis couldn't rightly blame him. The docs said he likely wouldn't remember some on the account of how much shock his body had been through, but then most of his silence, Davis knew, was likely the thought of dealin' with it all. Everybody handled grievin' differently, or so he'd heard.

Thoughts of momma, then Kenny, an' even Davis' close call only a week ago likely stirred in his brain like a can a coke shook up too much waitin' on an idiot. Davis was a lot of things, but the fella who was gonna try an' pop that top was the las' one on his list. That'd take what his ol' man referred to as 'a special kind of stupid', an' though Davis had been accused of havin' a bowl of it here an' there for breakfast every now an' again, he reckoned he'd leave bein' stupid to someone else for once.

To make matters worse, Davis had a feelin' a big part of the ol' man might blame himself, for both stoppin' to pick up Liam in the first place, an' for how Cheesy an' Buckwheat had it out for him. Davis didn't know a lot 'bout these sorts of things, but he could see what felt like a deep hole in the back of his eyes as they wandered off in a stare, back in some memory before Davis, when Kenny an' Liam had been younger.

Then, Jewels stood up an' said her mind.

Whatever had him bottled up cracked a bit. Didn't nobody expect that, an' while a great many folks had things to grumble 'bout after it all in the parkin' lot, it was like a switch had shifted in the ol' man, like a good few thumps on the top of the coke can before you ease the tab. Davis saw it in Allie an' some of the others, too. It wasn't 'til later that evenin' when they were at home that he finally slipped outside an' sat on the front porch to rock on the swing, a tea in his hand. Davis joined him in silence. The sound of the crickets, frogs, an' cicadas sounded like a symphony of the south around 'em 'til he finally took a deep breath.

"I treated that boy wrong all those years," he said. "Treated him like he'd done somethin' bad an' unforgivable, but the truth was I's tired of seein' him 'round 'ere all the time. Truth was I's such a mess-of-a-man tha' knowin' Kenny wasn't comin' back made me hate him 'cause he wouldn't stop comin' 'round. An' here all that time all he was doin' was tryin' to make things right by me an' you. All those years he felt like he owed Kenny or me, or all of them folks who'd been wronged an' hurt, an' we jus' shoved him away like a stray dog tryin' ta wag his way to a friend."

"Ain't no way you could've seen that, Pop," Davis said.

"Yeah, I know. But I cain't *un-see* it now."

"Then don't. See it an' be better 'cause of it." When the words came out of Davis' mouth, he didn't understand 'em. They jus' came from somewhere out in left field. It'd take more than few moments of the ol' man starin' at him like he'd grown another arm out his forehead before he finally nodded an' sipped his tea.

"Sounds like you've done some thinkin' too, huh?"

"Yeah, folks been tellin' me to use it for more than a hat rack so,"

"'Bout time, I reckon," he replied with a smirk.

Davis took a seat on the porch swing next to his ol' man, tea in hand, an' stared across the yard at the blue pickup sittin' in the drive.

"Well, what're we gonna do first?" he asked.

"I think I wanna start goin' to church," Davis said. "Not to be all fake or judgy, but to be a lil' more like Liam was — jus' good for the sake of bein' good, even when nobody else treats you right 'cause of it. Who knows, maybe we can get to know that Jesus fella everybody's always talkin' 'bout."

The ol' man smiled, noddin'. "Aight, what else?"

"We ought ta spend time with Kelli, too. I ain't never even thought of bein' an uncle before. I reckon somebody's gotta teach her things like slippin' firecrackers in mailboxes, shootin' a b-b gun, puttin' tha' clear wrap over the toilet, or hidin' a fish in a ziplock baggie under the seat in her Papaw's truck."

"In her *Papaw's truck*?" the ol' man said, holdin' back his sip with a lifted brow. "Don't pick a fight you cain't win, fella."

"Reckon we're gonna need to fix up the extra room all girly 'round here, too, huh?" he asked an' Davis nodded.

"Pink, huh?"

"Nah, pink camouflage," the ol' man replied.

"Best jus' let Allie at it," Davis said.

"That's for sure. We'd mess that up right quick."

"What're *you* thinkin' we oughta start doin'?" Davis asked after a minute in thought, starin' at the truck in the drive.

The ol' man slipped the folded papers out of his back pocket an' tossed 'em on the table beside the swing. Davis had seen it once before, when the executor of Liam's will paid 'em an unexpected visit.

"I've got some work to finish. Some store front shops to get up an' goin'. What d'ya say?"

"Sounds like we've got a lot of work to do," Davis replied.

~*~

Davis picked up Jewels from Allie's after school Monday evenin' an' drove her to the Fun Park to start her first day of work. Spring Breakers had finally finished terrorizin' the coast, an' with the normal hum of the traffic up an' down Beach Blvd. Jewels started to see another new side of the coast, one she liked even more than before, if that was possible. Allie brought Travis along, an' he helped coach her on how to run the rides like Liam used to. Davis went to baseball practice all that week, but decided he didn't really 'ave the heart to play anymore. He wasn't sure why, but the other things an' plans seemed more important to him. It reminded him of somethin' Allie had said 'bout finally stoppin' an' seein' life after all the go-go-go was gone that gave him a firm shake at the collar an' helped him see a lil' clearer.

By Saturday, he asked Mr. Montgomery an' got a job workin' the same schedule as Jewels all week, so they could ride to work together. Jewels used the time to tease Davy 'bout everything under the sun. Davis used the time to spend with Jewels 'til he finally worked up the courage to ask her out after a year of prayin' about it. He's pretty sure gettin' a firm smack upside the head from Mr. Montgomery helped, too.

By graduation, a year later, the shops finally opened. A hair cuttin' place, a daycare, an' a new mechanic shop was the first three. It took a few months before the other two rented out, but Mr. Allen wasn't in a rush. He was more than happy jus' turnin' a wrench in his own shop doin' honest man's work again. Allie's Daycare gave Jewels a closer job an' helped her have more time for night classes to become a stylist. The local junior college had a great program, an' with all the money she'd saved from workin' at the Fun Park, an' the account Liam left to her, she only had to apply for a couple of scholarships and was able to graduate with no debt.

They still went on walks, the three of 'em, whenever the weather was nice, through the woods, across the undeveloped acres clear to the river, along the paths Liam had worn down over the years. It made 'em feel like he was still with 'em in a way, encouragin' 'em to keep pushin' ahead, through the tough times.

Travis led the way one night, laughin' an' jokin' 'bout how Davy needed to 'eat more vitamins' 'cause he didn't hit the punchin' bag hard enough in the game room. It'd been a few months since they'd been to the Fun Park, busy with school an' with Davis helpin' his ol' man manage the shops while he was learnin' a thing or two 'bout turnin' a wrench of his own.

"I cain't believe I'm finna get on this thang again," Jewels said, shakin' her head. "I mus' be stupid, y'all."

"You've ran this hundreds of times now," Davis said as he opened the door, pulled it shut, an' slid the pin down to keep the door latch secure. It rocked back an' forth slowly. The look on her face showed her confidence in knowin' she'd operated it but ridin' it —that she hadn't done.

The ride started up an' around, the neon lights of the park buzzin' around 'em while the pinks an' reds of what was left of the sunset quickly faded into the dark blue sky. The distant islands came into view as the occasional honks and flashin' lights of the Friday night traffic on Beach Blvd. stirred to life. It wasn't too long after the newbie eased it to a stop with Davis an' Jewels at the top.

"Aw naw. Uh-uh. What's he doin'? I know dis fool bes' not be messin'," she said to Davis. "Ay!" she hollered over the side. It was only then she saw 'em.

Mr. Allen, Tamra, Terry, Chris, Angel, Cora Lynn, Ms. Luanne, an' Allie wavin' from below. Kelli an' Travis were laughin' together holdin' hands, jumpin'. The crazed expression on Jewels' face found Davis smilin' when she looked back at him, then down, to his hands holdin' the ring box.

"Oh no, you ain't finna ask me on this thing! Boy, I'm gonna. Okay, okay. *Yes! But* I'm gonna make some rules 'bout *this*," she said pointin' to the whole Ferris Wheel. "You take me on this again, for anything, an' we gonna fight."

Mr. Montgomery laughed 'til he cried.

About
Kharis Publishing:

Kharis Publishing, an imprint of Kharis Media LLC, is a leading Christian and inspirational book publisher based in Aurora, Chicago metropolitan area, Illinois. Kharis' dual mission is to give voice to under-represented writers (including women and first-time authors) and equip orphans in developing countries with literacy tools. That is why, for each book sold, the publisher channels some of the proceeds into providing books and computers for orphanages in developing countries so that these kids may learn to read, dream, and grow. For a limited time, Kharis Publishing is accepting unsolicited queries for nonfiction (Christian, self-help, memoirs, business, health and wellness) from qualified leaders, professionals, pastors, and ministers. Learn more at: https://kharispublishing.com/

Other Books by the Author

Follow me on Insta @m.e.reach

Website: https:mereach.wixsite.com/mereach